Passing Shadows

Anna Butler

GLASS HAT
PRESS

Copyright © 2016 Anna Butler

ISBN: 1540576531
ISBN-13: 978-1540576538

Passing Shadows

Prequel to the *Taking Shield* Series

Man is like a mere breath; His days are like a passing shadow.

Psalm 144:4

CONTENTS

ACKNOWLEDGMENTS

Edited: Val Hughes of Scarlet Tie Editing
Cover Design: Kellie Dennis, Book Cover By Design.

OVERTHROWN BY STRANGERS

Your land is desolate, Your cities are burned with fire,
Your fields—strangers are devouring them in your
presence; It is desolation, as overthrown by strangers.
Isaiah 1:7

WE'RE TWO DAYS out from Egereia when Earth goes dark.

Stop right there and look at that again. Make sure you get it.

Earth. Goes. Dark.

It is like someone flicking a switch. One minute I'm taking my duty turn on the bridge, feet up on a console, watching one of the news and entertainment shows that Earth beams through hyperspace to its colonies and ships, relaying them from fixed communications beacons through a booster to the next fixed beacon in the line. The next minute, the screen flickers and dies and Earth is silent. As if Earth is struck dumb, or I'm suddenly deaf and blind.

My first thought is that it's one of the *Sappho*'s systems. She's an old ship, and we spend a lot of time on maintenance to keep her going. It might be a faulty comms array, or we've twisted into a part of hyperspace where the signals are being bounced away from us by some sort of gravitational anomaly—a rare, but not unknown, thing to happen—or one of the fixed comms beacons in hyperspace has failed. I think about calling Grieves, our engineer, but she'll be sleeping and I'll look pretty stupid if it's something easily fixed. I've been around space freighters long enough to do some of the basic stuff. So instead of waking Grieves and getting an earful of grief for my trouble, I fiddle with the consoles for a little while, retuning the systems, recalibrating the comms array.

Nothing.

Sitting on the bridge for the hours with nothing to do... let me tell you, that is the definition of boring. Space isn't all it's cracked up to be. Oh sure, it's the ultimate frontier, the very epitome of wide open spaces, but the comms channel going down leaves you with nothing to do but stare at the monitors showing the muted reds and yellows of hyperspace matter writhing past you.

Very boring.

So, when the first transmission comes in from Mars, an hour after everything darkened out, I whoop with joy and almost fall out of my chair to get to the console to fine tune it in. Finally! Something to do.

And then I hear it. Really listen to what Mars is saying.

No.

Something in my chest stutters and shivers. Something leaden. Something that hurts, and no amount of rubbing against my ribs eases the discomfort. I try gulping in air, fast and shallow, forcing it against the lead lump that's trying to put a stop to my breathing. A hand made of ice closes around my gut. Sweat prickles at my forehead. Dear lord, I want to be sick. It's all I can do to hold it back, a hand over my mouth, acid boiling up like lava.

No.

Just... no.

I can't stop my hands shaking. All of me is shaking. It takes me two tries to turn down the volume and hit the internal comms system instead. I don't know what I say or how I sound when I yell for them all, but the Skipper stumbles in first, her sleep-clothes awry and a laser pistol wavering in her hand. Grieves is brandishing a three-foot-long spanner when she races in on the Skipper's heels, cursing a streak. Maeve is there, and Janny. Nicole and Edie, Tilly, Ford and Baum... all of them, alarmed and frightened, shocked out of sleep by what I screamed on the intercom.

"Liang?" The Skipper reaches me, puts a hand on my shoulder. "Liang?"

I know my mouth opens. I can feel it, feel the muscles tense to move my lower jaw, but I can't make my voice work. A wheezing, mewling noise comes out instead, no matter how I cough or how many times I try. That's all, just a mewling.

The Skipper's alarmed, her eyes wide and she glances sideways at the others. "Liang. Sweetheart. What is it?"

I point to the monitors and the comms channel, and turn to bury my head in her soft breasts, hoping to blot out the sound and sight of what's happening at home. She pats my hair and murmurs something, calls me her little bright one.

Someone turns up the comms channel. I can tell when the Skipper hears the broadcasts. Her breath hitches the same way mine did, and her hand on my hair is still.

When the clamour of voices and cries from the others die down to the Skipper's frantic shushing, we sit huddled together on the floor under the console, all ten of us, clinging to each other and listening. The broadcasts go on. We can't get away from them, can't bear to hear them, can't bear to turn them off.

Mars can see what we can't. They're close enough for their telescopes and scanners to pierce the millions of miles of space. They can see the blooms of immense light. They can tell us, voices hushed and strained with horror, of the boiling up of clouds so vast they cover entire continents and the crackle of lightning strikes so mammoth they're splitting the Earth and evaporating oceans.

We listen and weep, cling to each other, howling and screeching like the wounded animals we are. It's the only way we can share in it. We're trapped here, unwilling spectators, unable to pull away or put the noise and screams aside, witnesses to a catastrophic destruction. None of us have family back on Earth so we don't have as much to lose as some, but still it hurts.

Oh, it hurts. It hurts. It hurts like death.

Earth is just gone. No more. Melted into thin air.

Mars must feel it, too. Watching but helpless, aching with grief and anguish, battling the same incomprehension and disbelief that we are.

And then... And then Mars says...

"They're coming. Oh God, they're coming."

No.

No. Please.

Someone squeals, and the hands holding mine tighten until my fingers are all pain. Maeve is sobbing on my shoulder, turning her head against me, back and forth and back and forth, as if trying to rub out what we're hearing.

Because now the comms lines ring with dreadful calls for help that become a frenzied pleading, to shrieks and screams that are lost in the flat barks of immense explosions. All we can do is plead and scream with them, until all the screams, the noise, the dull percussions eventually stutter away into static. Into silence.

Earth is gone. Mars is gone.

I have no one left on Mars belonging to me, no family. We had scattered to the outer reaches of Earth-held space long before. My father died ten years ago and I left the vast canyons of Valles Marineris, never to go back. I'd thought Mars was behind me. Until today, Earth's Death Day, I have never realised how much of Mars is still here in me, memories twisting their way around my DNA almost, they're so closely entwined in who I am, what I am. And now memories are all that's left, thinning and drifting like smoke on the wind. The domed cities at Tithonium and Melas, the homesteads and farms... gone.

All gone. There's just silence.

When Mars is as dead as Earth, when the last newscast fades and nothing any of us can do at the comms board picks up even a squeak of a signal, everything is so quiet on the bridge that I can hear my heart thudding. The Skipper swears once and dashes her hand over her eyes, but she picks herself right up. She isn't folding, not just yet; the hand isn't played out.

We aren't going to fold either, that's certain. She won't let us.

"What will we do?" I clutch at her hands as she gathers herself to stand up. "Skipper... what will we do?"

"Divert to Daemon. It's the only thing we can do. Maybe they know more. Maybe they can..." She stops, blows out a shaky breath. "Oh Liang, I don't know beyond that. One foot in front of the other for now, that's all we can do."

Someone has picked up the universe and shaken it like a child's toy. Now it's upside-down with half the pieces missing.

All that's left is putting one foot in front of the other.

So, that's what we do.

You know, I never thought I'd end up on a ship like this. She's been a good boat to work on, and she's seen a lot of service in her time. I was lucky to get a berth on her. God must have been smiling that day last year, the day that the Skipper was looking for a shuttle pilot and I was looking for a job. Because if I'd been at home in Valles Marineris when it happened... well. We all know how that would've turned out.

The *Sappho*'s an old scow, wide-girthed and

blunt-nosed, built for carrying freight between colonies and occasionally running supplies out to a Pathfinder ship or one of the military outposts dotting the star systems. No frills. No furbelows. No luxuries. But for all that, she's a sound ship, solid and reliable. She's kept us alive all this while.

The Skipper owns the *Sappho*. Not outright, of course. No one person can own a ship like this outright, but she put down a good deposit when she gave up working for the Company. A few good years, twenty or thirty maybe, and then she'll own *Sappho*, the title clear of all debts and encumbrances.

"I flew scout ships on the *Sacagawea*," she told me when she was showing me over the ship after offering me the shuttle pilot slot. I was still thinking about it and she was doing a hard sales job to persuade me to take the berth.

The *Sacagawea*. She had been one of the exploring elite, then. After all, the *Sacagawea* is—was— one of Earth's biggest Pathfinders, one of the Company's immense exploration ships out there in frontier space, looking for new planets to colonise. Flying a scout ship on a Pathfinder made you pretty much top of the civilian tree. Only military pilots had more cachet.

The Skipper grinned when she saw my nod of acknowledgement. "It's not as exciting as it sounds, but I was lucky. I called in a potential colony planet in the Palatium sector that proved within three years of its foundation. It was a goldmine. The bonuses were..." She paused, and her grin broadened. She raised a hand and ran it along the corridor wall, caressing the steel trunking with gentle, loving fingers. I shivered, because I knew from the previous night just how gentle and skilled those fingers were. "They were good. Enough to let me retire and set up on my own."

By buying a two-hundred-year-old freighter. From a junk yard, I'd say.

Still, the Skipper hadn't skimped on the refit. The *Sappho* is sound and space worthy, and the shuttles the Skipper installed are little beauties. I daresay my eyes lit up when I saw them for the first time, because the Skipper laughed, pulled me in close and kissed me as thoroughly as she'd kissed me the night before.

I always say the shuttles sealed the deal. But it

may have been the kisses.

We made a decent living working short-term contracts, mostly in the Esquiliae sector, a good fifty light-years out from Earth. Not quite on the cutting edge of Earth's exploration of the galaxy, maybe, but frontier territory for all that. We hadn't explored much beyond it in this sector.

There wasn't much in Esquiliae. Half a dozen colonies established about a century ago, all held within three contiguous star systems, and Daemon Station, a large military outpost. Whichever of the Company's Pathfinder-class ships had found and claimed these planets, hit the jackpot that day. The crew would have been unimaginably rich with finders' fees, especially calling in a planet for military use.

Having Daemon Station nearby was a bonus for everyone. The service industries on Egereia, the nearest civilian colony, were booming with all those soldiers looking for a good time in their off hours. The benefits rippled out across the sector, and some even came our way. Egereia imported delicacies and luxuries from all the nearby colonies. We got to ship the goods in, and made enough in haulage fees for the Skipper to keep up the mortgage payments and for the rest of us to bank good salaries every month.

Good times. Profitable times. Hard work, sure, but the returns were worth it. We all worked hard, played hard, dreamt hard.

Shame it had to end.

FOR THE NEXT forty hours, the *Sappho* maintains course and speed for Daemon.

Scanners are pretty much useless in hyperspace but we monitor them for enemy ships anyway. Not that we have any idea what an enemy ship looks like. Who are they, even? What are they? We weren't at war. There had been nothing on the airwaves about running into any sort of new civilisation. We haven't a clue, not one single little clue, about what had really happened or who had done it or why.

Pointless as it is, watching the scanners keeps us occupied. We work in pairs: one of us monitors the scanners, another listens in constantly to the comms board for any traffic that will give us some idea what to do. With nothing on either count, I might add. The galaxy is shocked into a sullen silence.

I don't think, you know, that any of us is quite sane. We don't eat, or sleep. No one is ever left alone. We can't afford to be alone.

The Skipper holds us to our usual routine, a mix of her taking-no-bullshit and a softer cajoling that keeps us plodding along, doing what she said about putting one foot in front of the other. But I don't think any of us ever looks up to see where we're going. With so much death and destruction behind us, it doesn't actually matter, does it?

Just plod along, plod along. Bend our necks under the wheels of Fate.

The Skipper doesn't leave the bridge for more than a few minutes at a time. She spends the hours sitting beside whoever is manning the comms board, 'I'm just willing it to tell us something, anything,' she says in a rueful tone whenever I try to persuade her to go and rest. When finally an all-points broadcast comes in from Daemon, full of grim news and even grimmer instructions, she straightens her back, pushes back her hair and sort of rolls up her sleeves ready for action.

"Egereia is closest. We go there," she says to Tilly and me. Tilly is monitoring the scanner while I work communications.

I'm still trying to absorb it. Earth gone, and everything with it, a wave of continuing destruction radiating out from the dead planet. *Grab everything and everyone you can*, Daemon had said. *We're running.*

Tilly touches my arm. "Maeve's from Egereia, isn't she?"

We know what she means. The rest of us will never see our homeworlds' desolation, but Maeve will see hers abandoned. Maeve will know what the rest of us can only imagine, and I can't say I know which is worse. We resolve to keep an eye on Maeve, though, and agree we'll pass the word to the others—she's just a kid, the baby of the crew, and everyone looks out for her anyway.

"I... I mean..." Tilly stops, shakes her head. Her eyes are glassy with tears. She cries easily, but then we

17

all do. "They're coming after everyone? They want to kill us all?"

It seems to be some sort of cosmic joke, a reversal of the old creation myths. Only the gods are laughing, because this time God has thrown a stone in a pond. Earth went down, smashed by the rock, and the waves are surging out in a circle from its drowning, ripple after ripple after ripple.

Colony after colony.

If Earth had been created in seven days, it had been destroyed in seven hours. Now every hour brings more devastation. It isn't just Earth going dark. Whoever, whatever, the enemy is, their resources are unfathomable. They're implacable and unstoppable, ravening their way out from Earth in an ever-expanding circle, shattering everything in their path. So many dead, so many with no chance to escape.

So many lost to the monsters. The destroyers. The eaters.

"Devourers," I say.

The Skipper gives me a sharp look. Then she

nods. "A good name for them, love. A very good name."

She looks tired. Jaded. Worn out.

I lean over her and press my lips to her hair. "You need to rest."

"Later. There'll be time to rest later." She doesn't say that will be when we're all dead, but she might as well. "Set course for Egereia."

It takes a little while. While I drop the *Sappho* into normal space to reset the hyperdrive engines and plot the navigation, she calls the rest of the crew to the bridge and tells them that whoever's in command at Daemon Station has finally made a decision and humanity has a survival plan. Of sorts.

"We're going to run," the Skipper says. "We can't stop them."

Being helpless, being the butterfly caught in the spider's web, is sickening. She gives us a minute to cry and mourn, but we're all mostly quiet. Only Edie lets out a sob. The rest of us weep in silence. I can barely see the navigation controls, and my eyes sting like poison.

They've formed a sort of huddle, down on the

floor where we'd sat and listened to Earth and Mars being eaten. No one wants to be alone, and we ground ourselves and each other by touch; holding hands, or arms around each other, mouths against another's cheek. Connection, that's what's keeping us going. When I've put us back into hyperspace, I join the Skipper. She's in the centre of the group now, one arm around Baum's waist. I'm pulled into the huddle, held safe, and take her free hand. Her fingers squeeze hard against mine.

"Daemon will be the gathering point," the Skipper says. "We're to get as many people on board as we can, and rendezvous there. Egereia's the closest colony to us, and we'll head there and see what's to be done."

Maeve makes some wordless sound when she hears that, and Tilly gathers her into her arms, hushing her with kisses and caresses.

"Exodus," Janny says. She has always been the religious one amongst us, the one who prayed and read her Good Book. Not since Earth, maybe. No one could accept that as the will of God.

But now I can only nod and agree. It is indeed a

new exodus, with the whips of Pharaoh flickering their torment at our heels. "It makes some sort of sense. There's no going back, no looking back—"

"Don't say that," someone mumbles from the huddle of bodies. Nicole? I think it's Nicole, but it's hard to tell when everyone has their head down, staring at the floor, or has buried her face in her neighbour's shoulder. Hard to tell who's speaking when everyone's voice is hoarse with grief and tears.

"It's the truth. There's nothing left. It's all gone." I don't mean to sound shrill and sharp. Not with them. So I make my voice lower, softer. "If we're going to survive, it won't be here. All that's left is to try and live for as long as we can, and running away... yes. It does make sense. Run away and start again somewhere safe."

If there is anywhere safe.

But that I don't say out loud. I don't need to. Instead I disentangle Grieves' arm from around me and let go of the Skipper's hand.

"Time to make a start," I tell them as I get up. "We'd better go through the cargo and take out anything useful. Jettison the rest."

Ford pulls herself to her feet using the consoles. "Just jettison the lot."

"Not if there's food in it. We're going to need every scrap we can find." I glance at the Skipper, who nods.

"It'll be hard work." Baum's sudden smile is like a sun coming up. A faint sun, and a dire sunrise. Watery, as through a raincloud. "But it'll keep us busy."

And if we're lucky, get us too tired to think. And that, let me tell you, is a very good thing.

EGEREIA HAS PRIMARILY a services-based economy, servicing tourists from the richer colonies. Some even come—came— from Earth, all the way out to the frontier to experience the thrill, although they weren't just damn rich, they had to be astronomically rich to afford the fare through that many parsecs of hyperspace. All the big space cruisers stop off at Egereia to take advantage of the pretty coastal cities and the even prettier boys and girls. If I say that Egereia is the only one of Earth's colonies to have an official and licensed Pleasure Guild—that I know of, anyway, and I've been around some—you can guess what services are the bedrock of its economy.

There are half a dozen ships in orbit when we arrive, with more coming in, and it takes a couple of hours for us to sort out with them and the Egereian administration how we're going to play this. Daemon's orders were to evacuate and we can see for ourselves that it's the right call. Egereia has a few planetary defences but nothing compared to Earth's. And Earth had been snuffed out. Just snuffed out. Egereia hasn't even the proverbial snowball's hope in Hell.

While we wait, the mining colony at Actium, only five light years away, is hit in the middle of an evacuation. Daemon Station, when the Comms officer there speaks to us, tells us the planet is a smoking ruin.

No one got out.

His tone is strained, strident. "We're abandoning Daemon for a new rendezvous point. I've sent you the co-ordinates. Do a few runs and then get the fuck out of there, as fast as you can do it. They'll hit Egereia within hours at this rate. Definitely within the day."

Grim news. And we can work out for ourselves, thank you, that Egereia is in the Devourers' sights. It would have taken the *Sappho* around thirty-five hours to make the journey from Actium. There was no telling how fast the Devourers move. Faster than us, that seems certain.

We might not have hours. Certainly not thirty-five of them.

One of the cargo ships leaves orbit and runs for it, but the rest of us agree to try and at least get some people out. We can't leave them behind without trying first. Losing Actium puts the fear of God up the people making the arrangements for the evacuation, helped when a military ship, a destroyer, flashes out of hyperspace and her commander takes over in an instant. He doesn't take any crap whatsoever, sending down shuttle-loads of Infantry to clear the landing field and get it ready. He relays his orders to every waiting rescue ship. "Get those fucking shuttles moving! What the fuck are you waiting for?"

"We'll give it a max of eighteen hours. Then we go, whether the Devourers get here or not." The Skipper turns from the comms desk. The lights catch on the silvery threads in her hair. "It'll be non-stop, I'm afraid, Liang."

I pull at Ford's arm to get her moving. She's my co-pilot. She's a pretty fair back-up and doesn't warp under pressure. "We're on it."

By the time we get down there, there's enough clear space at the port for us to get our shuttles in, and we start the evacuation relay. Fast as we want to do this, it still takes time. We'll be hard pushed to get a run there and back under three hours. Pushed very hard.

I don't know how many runs the two shuttles make in total. Ford and I make five. Maybe six. I lose count. It's just an endless ferrying of as many people as we can carry back to the ship, push them out into the holds, and turn around straight away and go back down for the next lot. One flight, Ford takes the controls and lets me catnap. The next, we swap over and she tries to rest while I bring our cargo in. Tilly and Nicole are running the same treadmill in Shuttle Two.

I'd hoped I'd feel better, with something meaningful to do, but I don't. There are so many of them, and so few ships to take them to a dubious safety. There aren't enough shuttles to make a significant dent in the crowds of people down there, held back from the landing spots by armed soldiers lining all the fences. The soldiers are shoulder to shoulder, all the way along the inside of the fences. The military shuttles are parked ready to one side. When the Devourers get here, the soldiers, at least, might have a chance to get away.

Forced into lines to wait for their chance of life, the poor panicked people surge forward each time we land the shuttle. Even from inside the cabin we can hear the shouts, the screams, the voices begging us to let their children through, to let them through.

Every single time we land.

"Fuck," Ford says each time, quiet and dull. Like it's something to say by rote. "It's getting worse out there. We'll never get them all."

There's never any point in answering. I expect them to rush the shuttles, and each time opening the airlock doors is an exercise in anticipatory fear of just that happening, of us being overwhelmed and stuck on the ground when the Devourers arrive.

I don't know that in the place of those poor people behind the fences, I could hold back. I'm not brave enough for that.

The soldiers are in charge. They're good, I'll give them that. They have boxes of supplies and canisters of water ready on dollies for every shuttle that lands. The troopers handle the dollies as if they're made from tin not steel, pushing them up the gangplank at a run, manhandling them into position all over the floor of the cabin, pushing in extra crates and bundles wherever they can. Only then do they let the people through.

As the last load is brought in, the next group of people are already dashing towards us, the soldiers running alongside, chivvying them along, hauling up those who stumble and pushing along the ones at the back. I can't cram in more than about forty each time. Not with all those crates and boxes. Maybe a few more if they're kids and small enough to squeeze into the spaces between.

There's a moment of shouting, of shoving and

pushing people into place between crates, on top of bundles, of thrusting kids of all ages into the nearest adult's arms to cushion the poor mites a little on the take off. A wave from the officer in charge of our bit of the space field and I slam home the outer doors almost on the heels of the last man in.

Always the same advice as I push my way back to the cockpit and the pilot's chair. "Get down onto the floor as much as you can. Hold tight! It'll be a hard take off."

It's a blessed relief to shut the door on our tiny cabin, with only two or three people crowded into the cockpit with us. No room for more.

Take off is fast and savage, the whole weight of the world pushing us down, squeezing every muscle and joint, crushing us into our padded seats. The people in the cabin with us shriek and gasp where they're curled up on the floor. We don't take much notice. We can't afford to. All our focus is on just getting the job done and going back for the next load.

We save some time not having all the orbital and landing protocols to get through—we just speed down there, cram in as many food supplies as we can and then as many people around the stores as would fit, and speed back up where Baum and Edie wait to get everything off the shuttle and onto the deck in the shortest time possible. They've press-ganged some of the refugees into work teams to help, and turnaround time is pretty sharp after the first couple of runs. We get fast and slick with practice, freighting our human cargo.

Cargo.

Poor devils. Once they were just people, ordinary people, going about their ordinary lives, now they're refugees who are trying to cheat death. Old people, young ones, middle aged ones, teenagers, children, babies. Families that have managed to stick together and families that have been torn apart. People who are fit and hale, and people who I think we'll be better off leaving behind because they're sick or, God forgive me, old.

One trip, a man dies on the way up. Heart attack, most likely; he was red-faced and sweating when he ran up the gangplank into the shuttle compartment, breathing hard, with one hand on his chest. He doesn't make it through take off, poor bastard. When we reach the

Sappho, his wife shrieks and cries when we make her get off the shuttle without him. One of the other women lead her away, an arm around her shaking shoulders.

I space the body on the way back down for the next lot.

It doesn't make any sense to take people like him. They steal the place of someone who might have made it, someone who still has a life ahead of them. It's such a bloody waste.

Still, it isn't up to me. I take whoever the soldiers at the space field push through the shuttle airlock. They just send in the next in line, regardless, and I don't have time to argue. Well. I don't know that I blame them for that. I don't know that I'd like to play God and make impossible choices about who lives and who doesn't. It's just that I wonder about the ones we must leave behind, the thousands and thousands swarming at the space field who will never escape. I wonder what will happen to them when the Devourers get here.

We get out a few. *Sappho* isn't a big ship but we rescue about five hundred in the end, with thousands more on the other ships, before word comes that hyperspace portals are opening on the far side of the Egereian system, out beyond the tenth planet.

They're coming. Oh God, they're coming.

I'm half way back to the *Sappho* when I get the scramble code and hell, do I push those engines until they scream. Ford's beside me, praying and yelling at me to *hurry, hurry, hurry*! The Skipper will hold firm for us as long as she dares, but we have to get there. We have to. Have to. Hav—

I throw the shuttle into the deck, almost. Sloppiest landing of my life. The outer doors slam shut on our afterburners, and the instant they close, the *Sappho* breaks orbit and runs for it. Behind us, the hyperspace portals gleam blood-red as the Devourers come through in ships so vast they swallow up the stars behind them.

There are thousands of people, hundreds of thousands, waiting at the space field. They must be looking up to the heavens, staring up, squinting against the sun. Looking for a redemption that escapes them.

I'm not sure what we've left all those people to,

but I can imagine it. The soldiers will have pulled out to their shuttles first and got the hell out, if they can. I can imagine the crowds screaming, realising they've been abandoned, battering down those high fences and streaming over the landing pads, desperately chasing after the military shuttles as they close up and take off; men and women, dragging their children with them, crying and begging to be saved. I can imagine the cities under a pall of thick, greasy smoke, their streets alight and their buildings cracking open like eggshells. I can imagine the ground scorched, melting, the rocks fusing to dark glass. I can imagine the air is browny-yellow now, and the winds smell of fire and smoke and ash. I can imagine the great dust storms scouring over the ravaged land and tumbling the bones of the dead.

The planet is a goner, like Earth and Mars and a hundred smaller colonies. We humans are finished, and most of us are dead.

We're all dead. We just don't know it yet.

Ford and I sit shaking and sobbing in the shuttle's small cabin, clinging to each other, her hands fisted in my hair and her mouth on mine. We think we were alive, that we've made it out by the skin of our teeth. But we're dead, really. Walking dead stumbling off the shuttle and threading our way between the boxes of stores stacked on the shuttle deck, holding hands because right now all we have was terror, relief, a sort of guilty joy that we're still breathing... and shock and sorrow and more terror.

Tilly and Nicole haven't made it back.

The bridge is quiet as a dirge when the Skipper tells us, and her eyes are wet. She loves us all, and losing crew is like having a limb torn off.

Maeve is almost out of her head. We hadn't let her dirtside and she hasn't seen anyone she knows come out of a shuttle. The Skipper gives her a shot of something to calm her down and has Edie take her down to her cabin and stay with her. No shots of something calming for the rest of us. All we can have is a swig from the liquor bottle to choke down our grief and remorse.

You can't choke down the guilt. It sticks in the throat.

THE SKIPPER'S KEEPING the lights dimmed right down.

She's likely just trying to save power, because God knows we'll need it. She's already diverting power to the heating and air-scrubbing systems, and either dialling back secondary systems to a mere glimmer or wiping out third- and fourth-level redundancies altogether. Risky, maybe, to keep running with nothing much in the way of back-up, but better that than the power giving up on us entirely.

Grieves, our engineer, isn't getting a lot of sleep right now. She's running from system to system, trying to keep this old shit-heap of a ship in the sky. She isn't one to suffer in noble silence. She bitches. A lot. I've got some basic engineering training, so I get to assist and listen to the bitching. I sit with her in cramped service ducts in engineering or the water treatment plant, handing her tools while she carries out the sort of profane commentary that would make many a man blush scarlet. Being women, we have more fortitude.

But still, Grieves is worried. This is an old ship, with cobbled-together upgrades to her basic systems.

We're putting a hell of a lot of strain on her. So maybe power conservation is why we're all stumbling around below decks in a sort of dusky twilight.

Maybe.

And maybe it's more than that.

The Skipper's not stupid. Sure, we need to conserve power, but it looks like she's trying to keep a lid on things too, keeping everything on the down-low and calm. Maybe she read somewhere that low lights are soothing or something. Or she's hoping if it's dark enough, that the lost people down there in the holds won't realise how many we crammed into the storage compartments, and they won't panic about stuff like food and water and the deadly, deadly danger that we're in.

I don't think it will work. What they've got can't be soothed and it's not as if they can't tell by touch or sound or just by the goddamned smell how many of them we pushed into too small a space. We had no choice, and nor did they. Not if they wanted a chance to live.

At least the Skipper's kept them out of the crew's quarters. I only share with Ford and Grieves, not half the population of the colony on Egereia. Ford snores and Grieves has trouble with wind, but that's better than six families all piled into the cabin with us, elbowing their way into my space. I'm used to Ford and Grieves.

I don't like going down to the holds, not since we left orbit and raced away to the rendezvous point Daemon Station gave us. The Skipper goes down every few hours and walks through, talking to people and letting them know where we are and how long to rendezvous. That's all she can tell them: there isn't anything else. She doesn't like doing it, I know. She usually has a slug of whisky when she gets back topside, her hands shaking as she raises the bottle to her lips. I don't think she's scared, exactly, but there's only one of her and five hundred of them, and the minute they snap out of the grief and shock there'll be trouble.

I go down there with her the third time. She shouldn't go alone. It isn't safe.

I don't like going down there, but I do it. One or two got hurt in the crush at the space field, and somehow we find the supplies and resources to care for the injured, as best we can. I count three with broken bones, and one with concussion. An old woman has a temperature and is flushed with fever. She's disorientated and calling for a husband who isn't there; he mustn't have made it to the shuttle. I hope to God what she has is just shock and nothing catching.

There's a walkway that runs the length of the hold with the cargo bays, fifteen on each side, opening off it. Normally each one of those bays would hold cargo, or everything a family owned if we were shipping them from one colony to another. Now each one holds people. Too many people. When they lie down to pass the night in bad dreams, they lie in serried rows, each within an inch or two of the next. They look like the dead laid out, like a graveyard waiting for the tombstones.

Barely a day since Egereia and they've started staking out their claims, marking their territory with whatever they were able to salvage: a bag or a box here, a bundle of clothes there, and even, now and again, a length of fabric hung to divide up the cargo bay and give the illusion of a real division, of privacy. It hasn't taken long, this need for separation to come to the fore. So far, though, no fights.

They'll come. When they realise what lies ahead

of us, the fights will come.

Baum and Edie go with us, to help distribute what rations we have. In between helping Grieves with the engineering work, I've been working on a stores manifest. Even eking out the stores, the most we can do is give each adult a protein bar and make sure the kids, at least, get something decent to eat. Our hydroponics unit here is set up for a crew of ten and we can't do much with that. Even with the stores we've salvaged, that the soldiers pushed onto the shuttles, there isn't enough food to do more than keep the kids alive.

They take the rationing quietly. One or two ask if that's all, but they only grimace and nod when I say that is indeed all they're going to get until tomorrow. They're still quiet, subdued, too shocked to think things through. When they wake up, process the shock, then things will get pretty bad, pretty fast. At some point, I'm going to stop the Skipper going down there and batten down the hatches instead, no matter what she says.

Right now, the people in the holds are lost. Every last one of them, even the ones without a scratch on them, look... look shrivelled, as if they've lost so much that they're faded out, greyed over, the edges rubbed out. They're out of focus. They're less than they were before, that's certain, as if the Devourers reached down into every single one of them and yanked something important out that they can't get back. You can see it most in the eyes. Their eyes are wide and dark and old, so wide that sometimes there's barely a rim of colour around them, as if they're pulling the light down into them and never letting it go. As if they're trying to get back what the Devourers took.

Ghosts. They're still here, but they're ghosts.

WE ALL BREATHE a bit easier when we reach the rendezvous co-ordinates given to us by Daemon Station.

They were luckier than most of us. Daemon Station had an entire naval squadron posted there: a huge warship, with a dozen frigates and destroyers in attendance. They'll have got everyone out of the station and onto a ship in short order.

The warship, the *Alexander*, is in the centre of the squadron, buzzing with small attack fighters patrolling the gathering refugee ships. We aren't the first ship in and the soldiers have it all worked out, getting us into place amongst the other ships without fuss or delay. We're armed, although lightly, so we're put near a couple of unarmed freighters to help protect them if there's need. We all hope to God that there isn't.

But it's only a matter of time until the Devourers track us down. We don't have long.

They're coming.

I can't see what can stop them. Humanity certainly can't.

Still, we've made it this far. We're all glad to be here, and when the Skipper tells everyone, the ghosts look less thin and stretched and more as if they're really there, and there's even a faint breath of hope. We feel like we belong to something again. The comms traffic with the *Alexander* and the other ships reminds us that we aren't on our own. That's something. It's not all to our advantage, mind you, as the *Alexander* makes us squeeze more people into the holds, sending them to us from ships even more crowded than our own, but it's better than feeling that there's nothing but us and a hundred burnt-out planets.

I've been on the *Alexander* a couple of times since we got here, ferrying the sick old man and the three broken bones over for treatment at their medical centre. They took my name the first time I landed. They'll need shuttle pilots, they said, and added me to a list. We'll see what comes of that, if anything does. The Skipper needs shuttle pilots too, and I trust her.

They don't need me that quickly, it seems. It's two days before a shuttle arrives from the *Alexander* with soldiers on board. The Skipper calls me up to the bridge to take them around the ship.

"Li Liang," she says, with a nod to me. "My first officer. Liang, this is Major Matthias Harrington from the *Alexander.*"

We nod, but we don't shake hands.

"How is it here?" he asks.

The Skipper shakes her head. "We're a freighter, not a liner, and never intended to carry people. We have limited power capacity and I'm diverting all the juice I can to the heating and air-scrubbing systems. We have nearly six hundred people crowded into my holds and nowhere near enough food or water for them. We're lucky that there were so few injuries in the evacuation. Cuts and bruises mostly, from the take offs. Nothing really serious. They're quiet, because they're still in shock. Traumatised. I can't do much to make that better." She must have rehearsed all that, it came out so slickly. "We need help."

The soldiers have brought nothing with them although they promise supplies soon. Apparently a nearby agricultural colony is still there, being stripped bare by the military, and the agri-ships that carried their animals and crops to the colony are being loaded up to carry them away again. Rations will come, but not just yet.

Yes, that will really reassure the people in our holds while they starve and tighten their belts.

Instead of rations, says Major Harrington, they've come to carry out a census, get everyone's names. They need data. They need to know what resources they have within the refugee ships, what stores and people and skills they can call on. Oh, and of course they've come to assess what we need and to count both the quick and the dead.

I tell him that everyone's dead. They're dead inside, and dead in heart and mind. "It'll make the count easier for you."

The Major gives me a hard look, as if I'd hit him, but I don't owe him a thing. Instead I tell him that the hold is dreadful now, a place where grief lives and terror walks at night. "You can hear it in the nightmares when the sobs and screams filter up between the decks, and you can see it in the way the children are. They're so still and silent. All eyes. They'll never be the same again, they'll never be real children again."

The Skipper holds out a hand as if to stop me, and lays it on my arm. Her fingers are warm against my cold skin. "I know, Liang-love. I know. I see and hear it too. But it's no use. It's no use and we can only do what we can before we all lie down and give it up. But we aren't there yet. Not yet. We're still here."

Her fingers dig into my arm until it hurts. Her fingernails were once kept short and neat. Now they're ragged and torn where she's bitten them and her hand trembles.

It's all boiling around inside me, hot as lava, seething and pushing against my ribs until my chest aches. Rage and anguish, shame and guilt. All molten lead, weighing me down. Weighing all of the living down. When it burns up into my throat, I press my mouth shut hard, closing them against the words that would erupt out of me if I'd let them. If the Skipper would let them. She knows, and she knows how to stop me. So instead I let my head droop down and take a deep breath to steady myself.

"We're still here," she says again. Louder. She looks at me hard, until I glance up and nod. She smiles then, faintly, and slips her hand into mine.

The soldiers say nothing, but the Major looks away and can't meet my eyes. He looks drawn and exhausted; the skin is dragged at the corners of his mouth and his eyes are red-rimmed, and although I'd say he normally stands proud and upright, now his shoulders sag with defeat and the burden I've just slung on them.

The soldiers have so many burdens, what's one more? It's no more than they deserve.

"What happens next?" I curl my fingers around

the Skipper's hand and hold on for dear life. "What's the plan?"

The Major rubs a hand over his face, wiping away the guilt and regret, until he's all business. "The *Alexander* has scouts out in hyperspace, watching for any unknown ships. The instant we get the warning, we are out of here." He glances at the Skipper. "You should have had the course co-ordinates for our planned escape route."

"Received and logged. We'll make the jump into hyperspace as soon as we get the signal."

"I hope we get a few days grace, but I'm not counting on it." The Major's back to rubbing over his face with his hands as if to rub away all his problems. "Well, Miss Li, shall we start the walk through? With your permission, ma'am." He salutes the Skipper, bless him. As if the politeness matters.

He's brought a couple of captains with him and a crew of sappers, the military's engineering corps. He sets the sappers on an evaluation of the *Sappho*—this is an old bucket of a ship, and she's held together by faith and Grieves, who for all her intestinal quirks is one helluva engineer. Still, it's a good idea to give the old ship the once-over with better equipment than Grieves has, and Grieves is happy to show the sappers her precious engines. We leave her cooing happily and flirting with a sergeant. The Major comes with me into the hold. He gestures to the captains and maybe a dozen troopers to come with us, introducing the officers quickly.

He doesn't talk much on the way down, walking beside me and asking only the sorts of questions I'd expect: numbers, their state of mind, if they're calm or restless, how many injured, any sick? The captains walk behind us, the troopers in a well-armed mass behind them. One of the captains, the tall one—called Aronsson, I think—is as dark-skinned as Baum is, but not as beautiful. The other one, the smaller one called Kit or Kris Calvert or something like that, is quickness and light, like a gold flame. I get the impression he would normally be all smiles and charm and chatter, but even his fire is quenched right now.

"It's not good in here," I say to Major Harrington.

"It's not good anywhere."

I hesitate by the bulkhead door that leads to the holds. I really would rather not go in there again. "So far, the people here have been quiet. They're still stunned."

Let's hope they stay that way.

This is the first any of the ghosts in here have seen of the military since it all happened. There's more of a reaction than I was expecting. It's like something has galvanised the ghosts, bringing them back into focus from the shadows. They rush to the walkway, and there's an audible buzz of excited voices in the semi-darkness ahead of us.

The sight of the soldiers stirs the people up. They crowd into the walkway, calling and shouting, trying to get noticed. The soldiers try to be reassuring, but I can see they're not comfortable with it. Well, they've been found out. They must be embarrassed to be greeted as heroes when really they're hollow.

The joy, if that's what it is, is short lived. Things start getting ugly when people demand to know when we'll get more food and water, what's going to happen. Many of them bring their children to help emphasise

47

their demands, the children's eyes big in pale, pinched little faces. The parents are agonised, voices shrill with everything they've lost, with their terror, with the fear of what's to come. An entire damned chorus of demands for supplies, for information, for reassurance that we haven't been left behind.

I hang back and watch. The Major goes up a notch or two in my estimation. He doesn't take offence at anyone's cynicism, at the accusations of betrayal, of incompetence. He doesn't even flinch when someone at the back starts calling him a murderer because he represents the military who failed us. He doesn't call them ungrateful, unappreciative, selfish. He doesn't tell them to count their bloody blessings, the way I've been tempted to do. He's patient and civil, instead, explaining to them what's happening. They fall silent and listen when he tells them of the gathering ships, the numbers of people who have been saved.

"That's all? A few thousand? So few?" someone says, mourning and shocked.

The Major can only nod. He tells them of the plans to escape, to run for a space where the Devourers—he just calls them the enemy—won't find them. That yes, we will have supplies as soon as the agricultural colony is emptied. That many of his pilots are risking their lives scouting the emptiness of hyperspace between us and Egereia and Actium, watching for enemy ships to give the *Alexander* and the gathering ships enough warning to make their escape. That for now, the military is in charge, all of them answering to Commander Bekele of the *Alexander*, and yes, that means martial law will govern the refugee ships too. He's polite when asked the same questions over and over, and he doesn't lose his temper. There may be a decent man underneath that uniform. A tired and weary one, but decent.

A woman asks the question haunting every one of us. "Will we make it?"

"I don't know. We'll do the best we can to make sure we get away. The instant we get an indication that they're close, we'll be out of here."

There's a man close by, one with a discontented face and a sour, down-turned mouth. This one surely needs to be told to count his blessings and be thankful he's alive. The Major should try that line with him. "There's nothing—? No way we can stay?" He stops.

Grimaces. "No. I guess not."

"No," is all the Major says.

"Where are we going? Where can we go?"

Major Harrington rubs fiercely at his eyes. "To begin with, into the next sector, the Aventinus sector. I don't know what we'll find there. None of it's been explored yet, but we'll get as far ahead as we can in a single burst in hyperspace and then we'll work our way out from there." He drops his hand, and straightens. "I wish I could tell you more," he says, and his voice, quiet as it is, echoes through the hold. "I wish I could promise you that everything will work out. All I can promise is a hard time for all of us as we try and find somewhere safe. We're running blind and we don't know what we'll face out there. But we're alive. We're still here. It's my job to keep you that way. And believe me, ladies and gentlemen, all appearances to the contrary, I am good at my job."

He stands up, nods to his captains and gets ready to leave. "I need to get back to my ship now. I'll be leaving some of my troopers here to carry out a census, so we know who you are. Gradually, things will get better, and all I can ask is that you remain patient for now, and let the crew of the *Sappho* take care of you." He smiles at me over the heads of the refugees. "They've done a damn fine job of it so far."

They murmur and complain, but it's quiet and restrained and they let us leave. Maybe he's mollified them with his honesty, I don't know. I don't care, either, as long as it means I get out of the hold in one piece.

At the bulkhead door, Calvert waits. "Just in case," he says, when Harrington glances at the hand Calvert is keeping on the butt of his laser pistol. "I thought at first they were going to get mad, before your natural honesty charmed 'em."

The Major tilts his head back to rest it against the metal wall. "You can't blame them. They've lost everything."

"I lost a lot myself." The pain and grief cause crinkled lines around Captain Aronsson's eyes. "So did you, Matt. So did we all."

Calvert watches, frowning. I suppose I haven't given it much thought, but the soldiers must have had people they cared for at home, and who aren't there anymore. That's one heavy load of grief and guilt they're carrying, and now I'm sorry that I laid more on the Major when he arrived. Maybe he doesn't need any more burdens, after all. Maybe he has enough of his own.

"I know," the Major says. He sounds dragged. Weary. "I'd kill for a couple of hours' sleep." He looks at me, then, and I can see the redness of his eyes, the lines around them. "Do you think they'll stay calm? I'd hate to leave you with trouble to handle."

I shrug. "Hard to say. The shock's kept them pretty docile, but they're starting to get stirred up. We're getting hungry, Major, and we're all scared."

"Me too," he says.

Calvert puts out a hand that, in a just by accident, can't possibly have intended it way, brushes for an instant against the Major's cheek on its way to rest, in approved manly fashion, on his shoulder. The Major tilts his head to press into the touch. It's brief, but I see it.

The Major meets my gaze and I grin at him. I won't say anything. The ship's not called what she is by chance and I reckon he's looked at her crew and realised that.

"Thank you for your time and help." He speaks formally, almost ceremonially, as he straightens up. "I appreciate it." He shakes hands, and adds, "I remember your name from somewhere, you know. Have you been to the *Alexander* since you got here?"

"I'm a shuttle pilot. They put my name on a list when I was over with some casualties for treatment."

"I asked them to do that. I'm putting all the *Alexander*'s shuttle pilots back onto full combat duty and we'll need good people to replace them." He looks at me gravely. "Are you a good shuttle pilot?"

I take that as he means it and nod back, just as grave, but with the same humour lurking underneath. "I am. But I like it here."

"It's a good ship."

I grin at him. "We're the best."

"Yes. But we'll still need you." He smiles at me briefly and turns his attention to his two captains. "Time to go, gentlemen."

I put out a hand to stop him. "Major?"

He turns back.

"What you said in there about it getting better... It won't, will it? It will never be better."

He grimaces. "Everything we ever knew is gone. Dust and ashes." He takes my hand in his, and mine's engulfed against his warm, dry palm. "No, Miss Li. It won't ever be better."

"DID THEY GET WHAT they came for, Liang?" the Skipper asks, later.

"The sergeant's working on the census and they've got people checking our manifests, so I suppose so." I say. I lean my head down so it's resting on her breast. I can hear her heart thumping in its slow, regular rhythm. I'll get it beating faster than that before the night is over. I suck on her for a micron and smile when her heart rate speeds up. Her nipple tastes a little salty. "They might want me to go to the *Alexander* at some point, to drive one of their shuttles."

She runs one hand over my hair, pressing my head closer. The other cups my left breast. She squeezes the nipple, rolling it gently between fingers and thumb and I feel the heat start to pool between my legs. She has such clever, skilled fingers.

"Well, you're still young. You can't stay on the *Sappho* forever."

"We'll see," I say. "Nothing's forever."

"No," the Skipper says. "But we're still here."

THEY'RE COMING. Oh God, they're coming.

HABITATION OF DRAGONS

And thorns shall come up in her palaces
nettles and brambles in the fortresses thereof
and it shall be an habitation of dragons, and a court for owls.
Isaiah 34: 13

THE SKY LOOKS LIKE someone's tumbled a child's paint box across it.

It's all crimson and gold, violet and sapphire. Clouds, flushed with pink beneath, are billowing white and dark grey above the flat mirror of a long, thin lake.

Just above the steep hill reflected in the lake, the hill that looks as if the same 'someone' chopped off a chunk with a knife, is a patch of pale green, so clear and pure my breath catches in my throat. The landscape's desolation is lovely in a stark sort of way, but that sky is glory enough to make every heart ache.

There's something about it, probably the sheer inhumanity of it, that's a little bit terrifying.

You forget, living in a space-ship all the time. You forget about everything except how Earth is two years dead behind you now, yet still you look over your shoulder, wondering if the Devourers are back there somewhere, tracking you, relentless in their pursuit. You forget about everything except running. You forget about air that doesn't taste of old socks and last month's meals. You forget about how breathtakingly beautiful a landscape or a view can be, when all your gaze usually rests on are grey metal walls and grey metal floors and grey metal ceilings. Oh, you get a glimpse of beauty now and again, if your wall or floor or ceiling is on the outside of the ship and has a precious viewscreen to the stars outside, white and silver against a blackness so immense that the heart fails in trying to encompass it.

But for all that, it's a cold and colourless beauty, dull from its very constancy. It always looks the same.

The stars don't change while you're watching them.

So you forget. You forget about standing at the side of a lake, its wavelets lapping around your bare feet, as you watch a red sun set in splendour on the far shore while it sinks down behind hills as rounded as a breast and tips the edges of the world with gold.

Or, in our case, sitting in the pilot seats of a large shuttle, parked facing the lake, and staring out through the viewscreens at the spectacular lightshow outside.

I clutch at Alice's arm. "This place is having a very strange effect on me. I'm starting to think like bad poetry. Any moment now and I'll break out in blank verse."

"It's lovely." Alice tucks a strand of long, bright hair behind her ear and sighs. It's a happy sigh.

Her hair is the colour of polished chestnuts—at least, what I think I remember chestnuts looked like—

and taking strands of it and winding them through my fingers has made me sigh happily too. Not right now, because we're not alone. Being crowded by soldiers has me sighing with frustration rather than any gentler emotion.

So I take refuge in cynicism. "It's a sunset. I know it's pretty, but it happens here every day even when we aren't here to see it. And just because we are here, tonight, I really, really should stop with the romantic nonsense about it."

Alice wrinkles her nose at me, the way she does when she's trying not to laugh. "Liang. I'm disappointed in you."

I look up above the hills where the sky has created its own image of the lake below, the cloud shores and mountains enclosing bays of darkening indigo shot with gleams of gold. The lake reflects the sky back to itself in an endless echo.

I try to find something familiar to relate it to. "It reminds me of the Adamantine Coast on Egereia."

Alice stares. Frowns. "I used to live on Egereia."

I know that. I have no memory of her in particular, but she was one of the very few we managed to get out before the Devourers came when they rippled out from Earth to destroy all its colonies. I often wonder if she had been in one of the groups I piloted out personally. She always says she can't remember, that she was too scared to notice who her pilot was. I can understand that. I was scared myself.

"What I mean is, I know all about the Adamantine Coast. It was all resorts and sex and courtesans servicing beautiful people. Where does that fit with this?" She makes a wide sweeping gesture with her arms. There is no mistaking the disapproval in her tone.

Alice Russell is very young. She hasn't yet realised that pretty sunsets are all very well, but a well-trained courtesan is a godsend. She probably also hasn't realised that making sweeping gestures like that make her shoulders go back and her pretty breasts push themselves forward in order to be noticed, and that it makes me want to get her out of that uniform so that I can get my hands and mouth onto her.

She glances at me and smiles. Perhaps she has

realised after all. But the Major's only five metres away, and half the unit he brought with him is closer. Most of them listening in and grinning, the nosey bastards. Getting a cheap thrill.

"Adamantine isn't... wasn't just about being beautiful. Well, maybe.... But anyone could be beautiful if they had enough money and the sex was pretty damn hot. But the important thing is those courtesans had very well trained mouths and clever, clever fingers." Behind us the soldiers are shuffling and rustling and someone coughs. I hope it's discomfort. I don't turn around to see them all shifting to ease hard groins or see their reddening faces, but I can imagine it. That'll teach 'em to listen in to a lady's conversation. "I learned a lot."

"Liang!" Alice's face is as scarlet as the band of clouds on the horizon. But for all that she's smirking, and trying to look prim isn't quite working for her. The corners of her eyes crinkle and although she manages to keep her lips pressed together, she has dimples, damn it.

"As you know." I smirk right back.

"Ladies!" Major Matthias Harrington turns from where he's been talking to the techs. "If we're quite over the girlish confidences and you two are finished trying to make my troopers blush, there's work to do. We have a camp to set up. Let's get to it."

He doesn't look embarrassed. He looks like he's trying not to laugh. He has the same crinkles at the corner of his eye as Alice. He grins back at me when I turn the smirk his way.

I've got to know the Major pretty well over the last two years. I didn't like him much to begin with. Just after the Devourers came, we nursed our old freighter, the *Sappho*, to a rendezvous point with a group of naval ships headed by the warship *Alexander*. Major Harrington commands the *Alexander*'s soldiers and pilots, and came to *Sappho* a couple of days later to do a headcount on the refugees we had crammed into our holds. At first I didn't see how bone-deep weary he was, how tired of trying to deal as best he could with everything he'd seen and done. I was too busy making snarky little comments about how we'd been failed by the military, how we were all dead. I started to change my mind when he stopped a protest by the refugees before it could really start, just by being exactly what he is: an honourable man who wouldn't lie to them. Not that they cared about that; they were all desperate and dying inside with the pain that was almost too much to bear. They were just hunting for someone to blame. I'd blamed him too, back then, the way I blamed every soldier for not stopping the Devourers. I suppose I blamed him for not being dead, like everyone else. It was only later, when I was transferred to the *Alexander* to be a shuttle pilot, that I realised that all the soldiers and military pilots were as dead with pain as everyone else, really.

They just hadn't realised it yet.

There are still moments when the anger sweeps over me like acid, burning and twisting everything in its wake. I didn't have much in the way of family left on Mars and I hadn't been back to the solar system for years, but just the thought of it being gone, all gone and nothing left but ash and dust... well, sometimes there's nothing to do but retch over the 'flush, and sit there beating your fists off the tops of your legs, screaming your throat out.

It doesn't make things better. You learn to live with loss, but you never get used to it. Never. I suspect Matt Harrington knows that without being told.

Sᴇʀɢᴇᴀɴᴛ Vᴀɴᴇ ɪs ɪɴ charge of issuing e-vac suits. While the initial scouting reports from the planet didn't identify any threat from lingering radiation or anything like that, there isn't a scout ship in the universe can test for biological risks. Those are legion. First encounters on new planets are seldom with sentient life. We encounter sneaky little bugs instead. While there is a chance that taking in a lungful of this planet's air won't kill us instantly, it isn't a risk any of us wants to take. Not to mention that viruses and bacteria can take days or weeks to show their worst and no one wants to break out in something horrendous six months down the line. E-vac suits with a closed breathing system take care of most of that.

E-vac suits are close-fitting and the clear helmet fits snugly onto the neck seals to create my own little Li Liang environment. Struggling into the darn thing with Vane's assistance serves only to remind me that when we get back to the ships, we'll be so thoroughly decontaminated our skins will wrinkle to the point I'll know what I'll look like at ninety. Even then, we'll be quarantined for days. Weeks, maybe, if something crops up on the screening tests that the medics decide they don't like the look of.

We don't complain about it too much, beyond the ritualistic grousing. No one wants to have escaped the Devourers, only to bring microbiological death to the refugee ships instead. We've come too far, risked too much, lost too much, for that.

Exploring new planets has few rewards. Except perhaps the occasional glorious sunset.

WE CAME HERE IN two shuttles. We've parked them with great care, the main airlocks facing each other across only fifty feet of ground. Jerry Sheridan, the other shuttle's pilot, and I had a great deal of fun making that sort of precision landing, I can tell you. It isn't many shuttle pilots who could pull it off with our panache.

At that short distance, it's easy to co-ordinate the unpacking of the four inflatable life modules, two from each boat. Major Harrington stands between the shuttles, directing the teams of soldiers and techs carrying the gear to the campsite he chose long before we even set off from the *Alexander,* making his decision based on the maps created by the scouting teams. A slight bluff of rising ground runs along the lake foreshore, flat topped and level, a few hundred yards from the shuttles. We set up there, inflating the modules and linking them to each other with short docking tubes that seal to external surfaces and form reasonable airlocks. Barring someone jabbing the structure with a knife, it will give us a sealed living environment for the night. We'll still be breathing canned air, but it shouldn't bite us.

I spend an hour or so outside, working down one side of the modules to secure them with pegs through each anchor point, pounding the sharp metal pitons into the ground with a mallet. The gravity here is a little higher than Earth... No. How stupid is that? There's not much point referencing Earth these days. It's a burnt-out dust ball. So, all I'll say is that gravity here is a little higher than I'm used to. The mallet is heavier in my hand and I'm clumsier than usual in the e-vac suit. I'm very careful to make sure I don't miss a restraining peg and hit my hand instead. Aside from how much that will hurt, I can't risk breaching the suit.

So, careful does it, Li Liang. Careful.

As I work, the sun drops down behind the hills and the light fades to a dark grape-purple. Astonishingly the dusk has a scent I can smell even through the face-plate of my suit. It smells of sandalwood and something that holds tartness behind its sweetness. Lemons, perhaps. I think I can remember the taste and smell of lemons.

The instant someone switches on the searchlights to help us finish prepping the campsite, the scent vanishes. As the dusk leaps away at the coming of the bright lights, it takes the sandalwoody lemons with it.

It doesn't take long to establish the campsite. By the time I've reached the end of my side of the structure, and the soldier who was matching me peg for peg on the other side joins me, most of the team are inside the modules. When I've been through the basic decontamination procedures and been allowed into the main living unit, the soldiers are settling their bedrolls into position, claiming their space. Most have already shed their e-vac suits and are lounging around in shorts and thin tee-shirts. The women nod as I go past. The men, though, should know by now that I'm not impressed by their manly chests and the astonishing selection of tattoos they sport, but they can't help posing and flexing their muscles at me. I have tits and a vagina, so in their minds I still count as a woman, even though testosterone leaves me cold. I roll my eyes at them as I step over three depictions of *Mother*, each of them wreathed with hearts and flowers, to reach the module designated as our eating and recreation area. The owners of the tattoos just laugh.

At least, I won't have to share with them. Thank every god no one believes in any more, that dirtside protocol has the pilots and co-pilots sleeping in their shuttles, ready for an instant take off should one be needed. Alice and I will have some privacy, at least. Enough for my purposes, anyway.

I'd opened up the helmet when I came through the airlock entrance, but I don't bother getting out of the e-vac suit. I only have thin undies on beneath it, anyway. No tattoos. At least, none that say *Mother* or that I care to share.

Major Harrington gives me one of his patented serious looks when I come into the main module. This is the expression that has humour dancing underneath, where a casual glance or someone who doesn't know him might miss it. "I know you're pretty hot against gender-stereotyping, Miss Li, so I hesitate to suggest you and Miss Russell set up the field kitchen in case you yell at me."

"Which I would." I grin back, because I'm only *Miss Li* in that tone of voice when he's teasing.

"I thought so. Kit will do it, instead. And I hope you realise the sacrifice I'm making in the name of diversity and equality. After all, I've tasted the disgusting glop Kit produces from our rations." He laughs. Although we can technically never be off duty while we're dirtside on a mission, this is a downtime phase and using Kit's first name signals that the Major is allowing some relaxation. We pilots and his captains can stop twisting our tongues over 'Major Harrington' for an hour or two, and call him by name.

"Me, too." I pull a face just as Captain Kit Calvert protests in the background about the slight to his culinary prowess. His *Matt!* sounds rather more petulant than is seemly for a grown man, but actually, the Major's assessment is kind. Very kind.

The Major—Matt—turns back to me after swivelling on his heel to make an obscene gesture in Kit's direction. "Then we all suffer for our principles. You and Alice take the first watch, Liang. One hour patrolling the camp, seven hours off. And don't worry. We'll save you some disgusting glop."

He's all heart, that man.

WE'RE ALL UP AND around early, just after dawn. It's been a long night, several hours longer than standard. Cold, too, with cloudless skies, and by dawn the air is biting with frost and the edges of the lake are rimed with thin plates of ice. The land looks grey, bleak and dreary. The breeze coming over the lake brings roiling clouds with it and chills the blood with the threat of sleety rain.

Matt is back to being the Major this morning, all brisk duty and 'come on, there's a lot of work to get through here' efficiency. When he's sorted out the duty roster, I'm not best pleased to see he's separated me from Alice.

"Chief Engineer Hart says that the sensors show those hills may be full of minerals we can use and he wants to do some mapping." The Major glances at Jerry. "Sheridan, you're slated to take his team a preliminary flyover, and I want you to take Russell as your co-pilot. Hart has worked out a search grid already. Use Shuttle Two and check in every hour."

Jerry grimaces but nods.

"Sir!" Alice says smartly, and she's gone, running to the shuttle with Jerry to carry out the pre-flight checks. I must say she runs very nicely. Women often don't, because they tend to run with their arms across their chests to stop everything bouncing. I'm not big, but I bounce, and I hate running. But Alice is lithe and slender and she runs cleanly, like a young boy.

Still we had our shuttle to ourselves last night and Alice didn't need much encouragement to do the sweeping arm exercises again. What she has may not bounce, but they do pointing forward perkily very well indeed.

I give the Major a hard look. "She's my co-pilot."

"She is, but Shuttle 2's co-pilot is doubling up as the designated medic for the team exploring the lakeside on foot. I can't spare her to drive shuttles. Jerry Sheridan's a good pilot, but I'd prefer he had a second with him. I don't have worries about you flying solo. You're a much more experienced pilot than Jerry."

I suppose he thinks flattery will mollify me. I give him a look I hope conveys the correct level of scepticism, and he grins.

"What about me? What am I doing in my trustworthy solitude?"

"You're on my team—with Kit and Thom and a couple of troopers. We'll be checking out the city." Matt looks across the lake to the hills. Beyond them, according to the scouting reports, are towers and minarets poking up out of the vegetation. "And by that, Liang, I mean you can come exploring with us."

"Oh," is all I find to say. I hadn't expected doing anything so interesting. Shuttle pilots generally just act as drivers. We don't get invited into the action.

He touches the shoulder of my flight jacket. I had put it on over the e-vac suit to ward off the chill. "Leave that here. I told Thom to find you a protective vest."

Thom Aronsson is another of the captains. I've never quite understood how someone as dark as he is ended up with such a blond-Scandinavian name. Thom himself isn't sure, his family history twisted up with that of Jamaica, where he was born, to the point that no one's ancestry there is wholly clear, not hundreds of years after slavery was abolished. Too murky.

We're good friends, he and I. We were together for a little while once; just after I was transferred to the *Alexander*. But still being shocky from the destruction following the Devourer's attacks isn't much of a basis for anything permanent. Everyone was grabbing at whatever they could get, just to say they were still alive and prove they still had breath in their bodies. Thom and I proved we were breathing quite a few times before we realised what we were doing and stopped.

I'm biased, though, when it comes to what I want to grab. Thom's a great guy, but I still like girls better. Alice, now, isn't grabbing. It's a more considered and careful choice than that. Breathing with Alice is quite special.

But there's no time now for introspection about grabbing and choices. The Major's head tilts slightly and he frowns. He's expecting an answer, not me staring vacantly into space thinking about my sex life.

But a body vest? I'd seen the soldiers in them before. An e-vac suit is bad enough, but a tac-vest on top would be torture.

"Armour?" I shrug out of my jacket and follow him to the module where Thom is working, overseeing the fitting out of the ground exploration teams. Thom turns to greet me, a padded vest in his hands.

"Just light stuff." The Major reaches for a vest for himself. "It'll turn a knife and absorb low-level laser fire. Of course, it won't stop anything serious. If that happens, hide behind Thom."

Thom shakes his head. "He thinks he's funny."

"He thinks he's funny, *sir*." The Major raises an eyebrow.

Thom salutes, grinning, and holds out the vest

for me to take. "Smallest one I can find, Liang. You're bird-tiny, you know. I'm astonished we ever have anything to fit you."

I only shrug. It's been a problem all my working life, since uniform and safety equipment manufacturers appear to have only the lantern-jawed, tall Caucasian hero as their model. Anyone else has to have things adapted.

"All the scans indicate the city is deserted. Are you expecting trouble?" I let Thom help me into the vest. It's lighter than I expected, but bulkier than I like. It isn't exactly comfortable.

"The Major always expects trouble." Thom adjusts the shoulder straps for a snug fit. He has surprisingly deft hands for such a big man.

Major Harrington snorts. "Expecting the worst has kept us alive so far."

He isn't wrong there. We got away from the Devourers by... you know, I don't know quite how we managed it. They were coming out of hyperspace as we all fled into it, with barely the width of a star system between us. We ran for days, looking over our shoulders every inch of the way, before we came out of hyperspace again only to reset navigation and start off again at a tangent to our first course, something we repeated several times. Matt Harrington's skills helped keep us safe then, and since. I can live with him expecting the worst.

The Major looks me over when Thom's finished. "You'll do."

Kit comes to join us just as I lace up the vest, greeting us with an airy 'Morning, all!' He's already in his e-vac suit with the vest over the top, still unfastened and flapping about in a way that would annoy the hell out of me. He doesn't seem to notice. He's pulling a wheeled arms case along behind him and flings back the lid. The case is full of laser rifles.

"Can you handle one of these?" Kit hands me a primed rifle.

I take it rather gingerly. I carry a laser pistol when I'm on a planet, because if push comes to shove, I need to protect myself and my shuttle. The rifle is a lot heavier and more frightening-looking than the pistol the Navy issued when I joined the *Alexander*'s crew. "On a range. Never in real life."

"We aren't expecting trouble, but it if happens, just point it and wave it around a bit." Thom is shrugging into his own armoured vest and he sounds a bit muffled. "That usually does the trick."

"But point it away from me," Kit says. "We want to keep the body count down. Especially mine."

Charming. If he's not careful, he might make my casualty list.

THE PLANET HAD BEEN extensively scouted before the refugee ships even came into the system—the Major is a cautious man who won't risk lives unnecessarily. He always mandates a thorough preliminary reconnoitre before committing us to running any risks. Knowing him, he probably spent hours and hours going over the maps and photographs the scout ships were sent to get before deciding on his objectives for this job. I don't mind his caution. It keeps us alive.

The topographical and environmental data the scouts brought back suggested not much in the way of civilisation here: no inhabited cities, no power signatures. All the telemetry the *Alexander* gained from its high orbit drones and the closer scanning we'd done on our way in confirmed it. What little population is left is diffuse and scattered, nothing but a few hamlets surrounded by rough fields, with only a few dozen life signs concentrated in and around them. There's no evidence that the villagers have anything more technologically advanced than wood fires. No towns, no cities, not even the crudest of power production beyond that of our stone-age ancestors.

But there had been cities once, and roads and industries and power generation centres. Not any longer. Now there's nothing but darkness and destruction.

The city we fly over stood once in the bend of a river where it bent sharply to the south before emptying into an inland sea. I can't imagine what it was once like. All soaring towers and domes, perhaps, from the little that's left. Because although now the city looks small and broken, the bones are still here, visible from the air: streets, intersections, buildings.

On the edge of the city, the buildings are smaller, people-sized, and look as though they've just fallen down from neglect. Here in the centre, they're bigger and more daunting; roofless, great domes collapsed into themselves, or piles of debris, roofs and walls gone. The streets are gashed with great chasms cracking open across them, and vegetation is softening all the hard edges. Tall, massy growths, not quite trees but something similar with fronds like ferns, burst up along every street, hiding the smaller structures altogether. It gives the city the illusion of wearing camouflage, as if it's shy and hiding from us, not showing all of itself and peeking out from behind the covering vegetation.

The destruction stretches to the horizon, and even the river has boiled away, its course a dusty track winding through the ruins. From the level of degradation shown in the buildings, there has been nothing of this city but rubble for centuries.

Desolation made manifest.

IT TAKES US ABOUT TEN minutes to fly into the centre of the city from the point we first spotted ruins poking up amongst the foliage. Usually I'm the Major's driver, but I've been training one of the troopers, Penny King, as back-up. Penny is piloting the shuttle, keeping it a couple of hundred feet up, well above the topmost fronds of the vegetation.

The not-quite-trees must be a good hundred feet high, in places; taller than most of the ruins. The foliage is an odd blue-green with whatever passes for chlorophyll on this world. I coach Penny through a low-level pass to gather some samples on the grab arms fixed to the back of the shuttle, with a pair of troopers doing the actual catching. From the swearing drifting in from the rear compartment, they aren't finding it easy.

The analogy to fern fronds falters. When the two troopers bring canisters of their soft, slimy haul into the main cabin, it reminds me more of the long, ribbony seaweeds found in shallow seas on Earth where the water supported the fronds as they waved and billowed in the currents. Here there's no water to make up for the lack of a hard structure and the fronds are waving in what appears to be a stiff breeze. Goodness only knows what's holding them up.

The Major examines a frond using forceps. "Lovely stuff. Let's seal the specimen canisters and leave it for the botanists. Liang, keep scanning for life signs."

I do, but what there is, is sparse and unhelpful. No people around, that's for certain. You'd think some of the nearer villages would have sent in explorers and scouts, but there's no sign of it.

"Maybe they've learned there's nothing here for them. Maybe it's a religious taboo." Kit shrugs. "Don't care why, if it means I don't run into something carrying a gun. Or spear."

There are no animals, either, larger than mice or voles. Most curiously, there are no birds or bird-like creatures, no flying insects. Maybe wings didn't evolve here.

Major Harrington comes to stand behind me, to stare at the scanner results. "Okay, then. I don't see any reason not to go in. That looks promising."

He points to a huge, relatively empty plaza

where we can find enough clear space to set down, but he has Penny do half a dozen fly-overs before he orders us to land. Penny does pretty well, compensating for the wind shear as we get low enough to catch the breeze agitating the not-trees. She'll make a useful back-up pilot.

We sit in the shuttle for a few minutes, staring out through the viewports, taking it all in.

What surprises me is that this really isn't a very alien city. I'd have thought it would be stranger than this.

Oh, the architecture's different than anything I've ever seen before, but the architecture on the various colonies I'd visited was different to Earth. They liked glass pyramids on Mars, on Centaura no building was ever more than a single storey because of the constant earth tremors and on Egereia the architects had a thing about tall phallic towers.

Those sorts of differences are superficial. The form of the cities are the same. Here, as in any human city, is a central municipal area with huge public structures meant to impress, with the suburbs made up of the smaller buildings that, I suppose, people actually lived in. Just like Paris, or New York or London. Or Valles Marineris, my own home town on Mars.

This city is recognisable. Familiar. Comprehensible. A place we can understand, a place to empathise with, a place where we might grasp the rationale behind the buildings and the layout, maybe even work out the socio-political forces behind it. There's a sense that the people who built this, planned it the same way we would. Maybe had the same ideas as us about communal living, the importance of a cultural centre, a governmental centre. Had the same sorts of social structures. Or at least, had some social structure we could analyse and recognise.

Take the blank-windowed buildings lining the plaza. Windows. These people had *windows* letting in the light and air, the way we had windows to let in light and air. It's a tiny thing, isn't it? But in such little things, in such small similarities, the people who lived here feel like they might have been kin.

I'd have preferred something completely alien. This city is too like one of ours to be comfortable.

We're silent for a very long time, just looking

out at the city. When Earth went dark, we heard the Martian broadcasts of the attack, heard the despair and the terror. I'm willing to bet that every single one of us has jack-knifed up in bed, roaring up out of nightmare. We hear those anguished screams in our heads and imagine we're the ones screaming, that we're trapped there and dying in torment and pain. And I'm willing to bet we've done it more than once.

And now we can see it, or something close to it. This is what a desolate wasteland looks like, when war has burned across it.

I don't realise I'm crying until Thom's hand brushes over my face, wiping it clean. His own eyes are wet. I hadn't even noticed him swopping seats with Penny King, but I'm glad he's there. I tuck my hand into his and hold on.

"What do you think happened?" Kit isn't usually subdued, but the deserted, desolate city streets must impress even him. He's quiet and withdrawn and that's not usual.

The Major looks grim, his mouth drawn down so hard it looks as if nothing will ever make it turn upwards again. "Nothing good. That doesn't look like something that just fell into disrepair. It looks like explosive damage to me."

He points to a domed building at one end of the plaza. The dome is shattered, great shards of it missing, like an egg shell cracked open, the jagged edges biting up into a smoky sky the colour of ash. Rubble lies scattered across the stone pavement.

Thom shifts in his seat. "Most of the buildings show the same sort of damage."

"Do you think...?" I stop, shake my head, squeeze my eyes tight shut against the stinging. "Is it like this there? At home? I can't picture home anymore."

Thom's hand tightens on mine. He puts his other arm around my shoulders.

"From everything we heard and saw before Mars went, there won't be this much left." Matt Harrington's voice is cold, his tone a little distant. "This city is a greater memorial to its people than anything we have left."

"Don't!" someone says. One of the troopers.

"War, then," Kit says. "Looks like they're long gone, both the victors and the vanquished."

"Sometimes I wonder if we'd be able to tell which is which." There's a deep sadness in Thom's voice.

The city could probably tell. The city of the victors isn't likely to be this bleak.

The Major lets us mourn for a little longer, before he gives us all a metaphorical shake and gets us moving. "We need to get going, people. Our mission is to find anything that might be salvageable, any technology or knowledge we might scavenge."

"We're getting to be pretty good scavengers." Thom gives my hand one more squeeze and releases it.

Carrion crows. That's what we are here. Crows picking at the bones of the dead.

The Major's sigh is bitten off, as if he doesn't trust himself to finish it. He's a good man, is Matt Harrington. Duty holds him together. "We have a job to do." He glances at me, his gaze measuring. I'm not sure what he's looking for, but he nods and turns to Penny

King. "Keep the shuttle on standby, King, and ready to take off. Liang, you go with Thom and his group. Kit, you and your team are with me."

I don't know what I think about that. The shuttle's safe. Familiar. Going out there to look closer at what's been left behind... I don't know about that. It makes me feel that I'm lifting up my crow's beak to caw at the sky.

"Come on," Thom says in my ear. "It's good that you're getting to do more of this stuff."

Good?

Well, every yin has its yang, they say. The good stuff has a real downside here.

Thom checks the seals on my helmet and gives me a thumb's up. I return the favour and we go down the ramp together. Penny watches us go, her expression sour.

The wind is strong here at ground level, scything across the plaza. Without the e vac suit to block it, I expect it'd be cold. Something brittle cracks beneath my foot, shattering under my weight. Not bone, I hope. No.

Not bone… a cinder, maybe. The pavement is scarified, the surface glassy. But no, no bones.

"No remains anywhere that I can see," Kit says, quiet. The helmet blocks a lot and distorts voices slightly over the comms-link, but I can see his grimace through the clear faceplate. "Even if it was hundreds of years ago, you'd think there'd be something left. How long does bone last?"

"A good long time." Longer than I want to think about, at any rate. "Archaeologists used to examine bodies thousands of years old."

The Major shrugs. "They may not have had bony skeletons. May have been something else. Cartilage, maybe, or chitin or something we've never come across. Who knows? Okay, Kit, you and I will take a look over the other side of the plaza. Thom, Liang, you take the big buildings over here. Call in anything you find, and be back here in two hours. Radio check."

"Check," I say, echoed by Thom and Kit, and we part company.

Thom gives me a quick grin as we go to investigate the nearest big building, two troopers trudging at our heels, stoic and quiet. I try to smile back.

The building has a lightness about it, an airiness. The windows are wider than they're high, but they pierce the façade until it looks almost lacy. Delicate. I begin to wonder what holds it all up.

The doorway of the building is wide, too, but not that much taller than Thom. He can get in without needing to duck, but there's not a lot of clearance. The interior is all dappled shadow, with shafts of grey daylight stabbing in through the windows and a great gap in the ceiling where the roof's caved in. The light is cold and sombre, but with all these windows, I don't imagine it's always like this. It must be bright when it's summer outside and the sunlight is stronger and yellower. Cheerful, even.

We wander around the ground floor, stepping over broken stones and roof tiles.

"It's a library!" I say. The rush of surprise is woven through with a feeling of elated recognition. "A library!"

Thom agrees. "Certainly looks that way."

We're standing in a big central hall, the roof held up with sinuous pillars that make me think of the blue-green fronds outside frozen into immobility. Stack after stack of unmistakable shelves fit between the pillars, crowded with objects. In the centre is a collection of what can only be desks. They're a funny shape, long and close to the floor, short legged. They're piled deep in rubble. But many of the books—well, scrolls, really— are well preserved. Undamaged.

Over the next hour we check through the building. I don't feel the sort of excitement that would have me calling joyfully to Thom and the others at every discovery, but there's a solid satisfaction in finding more stacks of undamaged scrolls or rooms filled with what look very like computer terminals, damaged as they are. Thom assigns one of the troopers to stay with me as I explore. He carries the camera and takes hundreds of holopics, and he's almost as intrigued as I am when we decide to unroll one or two scrolls to photograph.

"Do you reckon anyone will mind if I keep one?" he asks, positioning the unrolled scroll on one of the long, low desks, to catch the best light

I glance at the rubble and dust. Somewhere, far

off, I can hear the dripping of water through the broken roof. "I don't think there's anyone left to care."

He grimaces, and slips one into his pack along with the camera.

The scrolls appear to be made of sheets of a thin, flexible metal, covered in a dense cuneiform text and scattered with little jewel-like illustrations in bright colours that catch the light. I keep one open to show Thom when we meet up again near the entrance.

"This looks like gold leaf." I point to illustrations of strange mythical beasts. At least they look mythical to me. They're probably the local equivalent of cats and dogs. "Look. Pity we can't read any of it."

"Matt will like those," Thom says. "It's the sort of thing that interests him. The linguists might be able to make something of them, too. We'd better take a few back."

I push a dozen or so into my backpack, taken from different areas in the stacks. I hope I've got a good range of books: literature or poetry, biography and maybe even textbooks. I'll keep one for myself, I think.

As a memorial.

The second building we try is less comprehensible. The rooms are smaller than the library and many don't have anything that I'd confidently describe as furniture. Most are empty, but for dust.

"No idea," I say when Thom seeks my opinion. The two troopers just shrug. There's nothing here to catch the attention.

We go back out into the plaza. Total sum of knowledge gained: these people had libraries and valued thought, taking care to record it. They had some things we can recognise, and some we can't. None of which might help the refugee ships find a new place to call home, far from the ravages of the Devourers.

And it's starting to rain. Dark grey clouds thicken over the broken, jagged rooftops, and big drops of water splash onto the pavement, leaving teary stains. Across the plaza the blue-green fronds stiffen and reach upwards. They look as they're putting up arms to pull the clouds and rain into a close embrace.

Kit appears in the doorway of the building he and the Major were looking at and waves us all over, calling us all on the radio. "King can come, too. This place is deserted."

No danger, he means. I hope he's right.

"I think we got a museum or an art gallery," he says when we join him. Penny King is puffing along behind us, hurrying to catch up. Running in an e-vac suit and tac-vest isn't fun. "What about you?"

Thom shrugs. "Pretty sure that one building is a library. We have no idea about the other one. No sign of people."

"I've got some books for Matt," I say. "Scrolls, really."

Kit rolls his eyes. "You don't have to suck up to the Major, Liang. He already likes you."

Thom catches at his arm. "No sign of people, Kit. And I mean no sign at all. No bodies, no organic matter."

"No sign in here either. Maybe they all evacuated, before whatever it was happened. Maybe it's like the Major said, and they were made of something less durable than calcium, less tenacious, and they've weathered away to nothing." Kit raises both hands in a *how should I know?* gesture "If we find anything at all, the biologists can come up with a theory. Anyhow, come and take a look at our art. It's pretty interesting."

The Major is in a long gallery, the windows shuttered so tight that, Kit explained, they hadn't been able to open them. The pool of golden light from the Major's flashlight illuminates a painting of some sort. He glances round when we join him, his face shadowed in the dim backwash from his flashlight.

The pool of light goes from painting to painting. The people in the paintings don't really look human: they're almost as broad as they're high, and they're hairy. They have heads and arms and legs, so they're the right sort of shape, I suppose, but their faces aren't... well, they don't look much like faces.

"They're a wee bit vertically-challenged," Thom says.

"And overcompensating horizontally." But Kit doesn't sound as if his heart is in the banter.

It explains the low desks, the doors and windows that are wider than they're tall. It fits.

"They're sort of human-ish." The Major sounds strange, as if something's stolen his breath. And he sounds cold. "More than just a human sort of shape or because they built a recognisable sort of city, I mean."

I see what the Major's getting at and what's put that odd note in his voice. The real problem isn't that the people of this place are only human-like and not human, that they weren't very tall and were very broad instead. The real problem is that you could have put these paintings into any gallery on any of Earth's colonies that you care to name and what they represented would be instantly familiar.

These are domestic scenes. They are scenes of homes, dwellings of some sort, with the people who lived in them. Scenes that had to be parks or gardens, where people lounged on blue-green grass and smaller versions of themselves ran about nearby. A procession. Something that might have been a dance or festival, with the participants wearing ribbons that the artist had caught fluttering in a breeze. Families. Couples. Several portraits of dignitaries or leaders, looking solemnly out at us, weighing us up. Finding us wanting.

The people in the paintings had lives and

families and did the same sorts of things that people back home had done before the Devourers came, when we still had lives and families and homes. We can all see it.

The Major's face is set. Kit's voice trails away into nothing. Penny and several of the troopers are swearing softly to themselves. Thom's turned his face away from us and all I can see in the gloom is the back of his head.

"I think that they must have been like us in the ways that matter," I say, after a few minutes, just to break a silence that weighs on me, that's clinging to me like a second skin, smothering me over.

Thom nods. "Yeah."

Kit says, very quietly, "They were born and lived and... loved, do you think? I think they did. Those two there, they're holding... well I was going to say holding hands, but they're holding whatever they had instead of hands. It might not mean anything really, but..."

"I think it does. I mean..." I hunt for words, as hesitant as Kit was, and I force every one of them past the lump at the back of my throat. "They don't look very human. But if they weren't like us, and living and loving weren't important, then why would they paint this stuff? I think you only do that when you know that it's the most important thing there is and you preserve it for other people to see, to show them how you lived and loved and who you were."

"People like us." Thom nods again. His eyes glint in the dusky light as he turns towards me, before shadow creeps over them again.

"And just like us, they die. They live for a little while, and then it's all over and there's no coming back." The Major looks up towards the ceiling. I can't see his face well enough in the dim light to make out his expression, but there's a tremor in his voice, a note of aching sorrow. "All the lights go out."

"I wonder what happened to them," I say, and I can hardly recognise my own voice.

The Major's voice is low and harsh, bitter as death as he turns all our words on their heads. "People like us happened to them, probably."

We all stare at him.

"It was one of two things, wasn't it?" he says in that same cold voice, the sort where the tremors lurk under the smooth surface. "War and battle and destruction happened here. Either people like us, warriors and soldiers, did it to them because they were the enemy. Or the people like us, those noble warriors and brave soldiers, were failures and let their enemies walk all over them and destroy them, the way we let the Devourers destroy us. The way we failed."

"Matt—" Thom says, his voice breaking on the word.

The Major shakes his head and turns away. "I used to love the National Gallery in London. The one in Trafalgar Square. Did any of you know it?" He stops and no-one dares say anything. He says, very quietly, "The lights are out there too, I guess."

"I think some of that's right," Kit says. "Something bad happened here. But Liang's right, too. If they were like us in the ways that count, then what matters isn't that they're gone, but that they were here at all." He grimaces. "Lords, that sounds trite. You know what I mean."

He meets Thom's gaze and jerks his head towards the door.

Thom takes my hand in his. He turns to the troopers and gestures to them all to leave. "Why don't we take a look around on another floor?" he murmurs and pulls me towards the door, shepherding the soldiers out before us.

I don't need to be pushed and pulled, actually, since I'm not stupid.

At the door, I pause and glance back. There's a pool of light where the Major and Kit stand, and Kit is talking earnestly. I can't hear what he's saying. The Major has his head bent and he isn't saying very much but he nods once. Kit puts out one hand and rests it against Matt's faceplate as if he could touch Matt's cheek with it; his other hand is resting on Matt's shoulder. Matt bows his head to rest against Kit's, as though mouth is reaching for mouth. He goes into Kit's arms as if to his rest.

I turn away quickly. I wasn't meant to see that. Nobody was meant to see that. I pretend that I didn't.

THE RAIN CLEARS BY mid-afternoon and tonight's sunset is as glorious as yesterday's. One of the techs tells me that it's probably normal around here to have spectacular sun-downs, and whatever happened here to this planet and its people did something to the atmosphere and the weather patterns and these magnificent skies are the result. Maybe before the destruction here, the sun went down behind the hills and nobody remarked on it because the evening just got dark without the sky being painted first. It would be a shame to miss out on sunsets like these, but I guess it would depend on your perspective. Losing your entire world to get a pretty sunset, to get such beautiful light before the darkness comes... that's quite a sacrifice.

Mars used to have pretty sunsets, too.

Alice and I stand to watch this one. She's seen the books and the few pictures we brought back with us, and she's been as quiet as me ever since. Everyone is quiet. Earth is only two years dead, after all. The grief is very near tonight.

Thom comes up behind me. "Nice," he says,

with a nod at the sky.

Tonight there's more violet and indigo and the vulnerability of pale spring green. It's very nice. It makes something in my chest hurt again.

After a moment, he says, "Matt's a bit hampered by that conscience of his. His dad was a bishop, did you know? Church of England or something. Really traditional stuff. Matt says the religious imprinting is pretty hard to get rid of it." He glances at me. "Not that Matt's still very religious, of course."

Not many people are. Not after what they've lived through.

"It's stupid blaming yourself for the Devourers, though."

"I don't think he does, not really. Matt just doesn't like failure." He grins at me, but there's a sadness to the way his mouth twists. "Kit can deal with him better than anyone."

I see the look in his eyes then. Oh Thom. Poor Thom.

"I know. Kit's the right antidote for a religious

upbringing. He's like an inoculation against guilt." I try to grin back at him. "But not against sin."

He looks alarmed, because he knows what I saw. "Liang—"

"Matt doesn't like failure and he's a very private man. I know. I won't say anything."

Thom smiles and puts his arms around me and struggles to rest his chin on the top of my helmet for a minute before giving me a little shake. He laughs softly, presses his faceplate against mine in lieu of a kiss to my cheek and pats Alice on the shoulder before going back to patrol the camp. He and his team have the watch. Matt walked off down the lakeshore half an hour ago and Kit followed him. They're nowhere to be seen, but just before he turns away, Thom looks after them anyway.

I don't think it's Kit he's looking for.

Poor Thom.

I haven't told Alice about Matt and Kit. Alice looks at me, a half-smile visible, and I realise I don't have to say anything. She's smart enough to have picked it up on her own. Instead, we watch the sun sink into the hills beyond the lake.

"I was thinking how everything comes to an end." I look at the sun. "They watched it once, the people who lived here, ached over how lovely it is the way we do, and now they're gone and left no one to see the sun. We'll see it for two or three nights but we'll be gone in a couple of days, and there will be no one left. It will come back, day after day, for thousands of millions of years. And no one's heart will ache to see it."

"Still, at least we've seen it," Alice says. "And at least we're seeing it right now."

She comes a little closer, her hand slipping into mine, and we watch the sun go down.

WINTERLIGHT

*Which hope we have as an anchor of the soul,
both sure and steadfast*
Hebrews 6:19

UNTIL TWO OR THREE years ago, I wouldn't have got within fifty metres of the bridge of the *Alexander*, Earth's last warship, much less have a work station on it. Well, so far as we know it's Earth's last warship. We certainly haven't run into any others and since there's no Earth left to dispute the claim, I'll go on making it.

I'm not sure that I'm qualified to do bridge duty, to be honest, but I didn't get a choice. I got drafted. Major Mathias Harrington might be military, but he's not blind to talent elsewhere when he finds it and he's quite ruthless about putting it to use.

I've been on his team for almost five years now, ever since... well, ever since Earth. I started out driving shuttles, and then that evolved into always driving the Major's shuttle whenever he was going somewhere amongst the refugee ships or, more excitingly, whenever he and his troopers were exploring the new worlds we came across in our long journey. After a little while, I wasn't just driving shuttles but became a real member of his team, allowed to get out of the shuttle and walk around poking my nose into whatever it was the Major needed charted or explored or analysed. A year later that morphed again. Sure, I'm still on his exploration team, but the day job now is transport logistics. I don't just drive his shuttle. I manage every damn shuttle on every damn ship in this refugee fleet.

I did register a complaint about all the extra work, but the Major has a habit of motivating you through disappointment. And by that, I mean we all do anything we can to avoid disappointing him. He merely has to look as though puppies are being kicked before his eyes and we fall over ourselves to placate him. He looked pained when I suggested I wasn't really management material, and I found myself babbling reassurance, that of course I was fine with it, just apprehensive.

He wasn't exactly empathetic to my concerns. "It's promotion, Liang. Of a sort. But most of all it's a criminal waste to keep you as a shuttle driver. You were first officer on the *Sappho*, weren't you? You know how to get shit done. The shuttles are a mess, the drivers are demoralised and scheduling is a joke. Sort the crap out."

I took it as a vote of confidence and, as directed, I sorted crap, banged various heads together and earned myself a seat where all the great and good lived, up on the 'top floor' with the management. And there I remain.

It is, of course, an honour.

/end sarcasm.

AMBER ALERT KLAXONS HAVE only one advantage over the red variety: they're a lower frequency and don't give me as bad a headache. But that's not much of a consolation when there are lights flashing and klaxons blaring, and orders being yelled at the bridge desks monitoring *Alexander*'s various defensive and offensive systems. Everyone, even me, has a job to do here. I'm recalling all shuttles to their ships: *no arguments, no delays, haul your arse back to the barn at top speed.* The others are doing things more directly connected to the ship's safety—weaponry, getting all fighter ships in the tubes and their pilots ready to go, manning defensive gun turrets, environmental, shielding, engineering… all the big stuff.

Shit is heading our way. Possibly very bad shit.

Alexander has the strongest deflective shields Earth's technology could devise. They're online within a second, the grid of emitters built into her hull energising to close the shields over her in a network of cold violet-blue light, lines arcing from emitter to emitter.

"Weapons systems on line. Standby," Lt. Commander Benson, the Exec Officer, says from the command chair. "Comms desk, alert all the other ships and order them to designated defensive positions."

Translation: 'Tell them to cower behind us and pray.' Most of the ships carrying refugees from the Devourer attack are only lightly armed.

The Defence desk officer cuts in with "Shields one hundred percent, sir!"

Benson acknowledges that with a nod. The rest of us sag in our chairs in relief. Until five years ago, the received wisdom was the shield would hold against most forms of attack. After the Devourers, we aren't so darn cocky. It may be an illusory sense of safety, but this is all we have.

"What's up, sir?" Major Harrington comes out of the bridge elevator running. Benson gets up and meets him at the Comms console only a few feet away from me.

Benson and I don't like each other. He doesn't think the refugee ships need a transport logician, despite my having proved I can get results. Or perhaps it's just he doesn't think the transport logician should be me and stationed on his bridge. Or because I have a womb. Who knows? He got overruled by the Commander, and here I am. He's never quite forgiven me for that.

He's a fussy little man with a horrible habit of dabbing his hands at you while he's talking, looking earnestly into your eyes while his hands make patting motions on your arm. He only did it to me the once. In my case, dabbing is by invitation only, and Benson's the sort whose hands will sort of slip towards your tits if you get distracted by the earnest looks and let him. I don't let him. One of these days, there's going to be a shuttle accident and he'll be a sad, sad casualty. I have it all planned out. I suspect even Matt Harrington will look the other way, and not just because it will be his only chance of promotion.

"The forward scouting patrol started picking up audio-visual transmissions as soon as they did the jump into the next system. The transmissions are genuine, in a language or frequency we haven't come across before." Benson dabs at the Major's arm with one hand and waves the other towards the data screen at the telemetry desk. "We sent the patrol in to check it out, slow and careful, in the hope they can pick up on visuals and relay it back to us. So far, no luck."

The Major takes a half-step to one side to get out of reach. "Kit Calvert's patrol? Calvert's good at handling first contact."

"Yes. He's having problems relaying the stuff to us, at the moment. We're just a little too far away and there's no comms booster in position."

Benson sounds faintly accusatory, but he knows we're rationing tech now. Stuff like comms relay boosters are no longer ten a penny, not now the companies that used to produce them for the military went up in the same smoke as Earth. *Alexander*'s engineers have set up production lines for tech hardware on the various ships in the fleet, but both productivity and quality can't yet match what we used to have. The Major's teams are less wasteful than they used to be with their toys, and Benson knows it. The situation isn't helped by the demands of the 'alert' protocol: we must slow the *Alexander*, put some distance between us and potential threat. That isn't going to help Kit relay scanner readouts and analysis to us.

Major Harrington nods. "Standing orders are to send back one of his patrol to act as a signal booster."

"That's been done." Benson waves a hand at the screens. "Blue-2-2 is on her way. Should be in position in a few minutes."

"Good. We need that data." The Major glances around. "What's the system configuration?"

The bridge can't just have one captain. It has to have sub-captains too. Redundancy is all, to the military mind. One of the redundancies speaks up. "Seven planets all told, sir. The inner planet is a small, barren rock with no discernible atmosphere. The outer five are

111

gas giants, all with systems of captive moons of varying sizes, some with very erratic orbits. The second planet, about three-quarters of the size of Earth, is the one of interest. Initial scans indicate a silicate rock crust surrounding a molten iron or iron-sulphide core. Oxygen-rich atmosphere. The transmissions originate there."

"Technology level?"

"Sophisticated, so far as we can tell from this distance. From Calvert's report, they've certainly got a planetary defence grid that seems to be the equal of anything we had."

The Major snorts. "For their sakes, I hope it's more effective."

Because nothing had stopped the Devourers who came to eat Earth. Nothing.

Benson grimaces. "For our sakes, I hope it's not."

It pains me to admit he has a point.

Benson continues talking to Harrington. "The Commander was on her way back from visiting one of the factory ships when the patrol's message came through. She's still en route. We've alerted her and we're briefing her all the way. ETA about ten minutes."

That's my job, to get her back. "Eight," I say. "The shuttle's been ordered back at top speed." I glance at the monitor when the Defence desk pings me with the data I need on the shield. "I'm sending the pilot the shield harmonic frequencies and keying the shuttle into all modulations."

Because it will piss off Commander Meseret Bekele no end if her shuttle bounces off the shields and she can't land. I don't want to be here when something like that happens. Bekele takes no prisoners.

The Major's not fazed by her imminent arrival. "We've run so many combat drills, we're ready for this. Everyone knows what to do. No reaction to our presence or the scans Calvert's patrol has done?"

Benson glances at the bridge sub-captain who'd chimed in earlier.

The sub's on the ball. An unusual occurrence, believe me, but I suppose having the Commander on the other end of a communications link is… energising, shall we say. "They're sophisticated enough to be able to detect intruders into their system, Major. Captain Calvert reported that his patrol has been scanned. But nothing more substantive than that. We've got Calvert monitoring, of course."

"Of course," Harrington says, dry as dust.

The sub-captain shrugs and moves away to the sensor desk.

Telemetry has the system map up on the main screen. Harrington studies it for a few moments. "I'll send in another patrol from the other side to see what's there. They'll be hidden by the sun and out of reach of the planet's scanners and the planetary defence system, but they can support Calvert if needed. A moment, sir…" He leans over me. "Scramble all the infantry transports too, Liang. Just in case."

He talks briefly with whoever's managing the duty office at the moment, getting more fighter ships into the air and the infantry contingent prepped and ready. "Who's in the tubes? Right. Immediate launch and take an elliptical course to co-ordinates…" He jogs over to the Telemetry desk and traces a route on the screen with a forefinger. "To alpha-7-T90-mark205-zeta54. Drop a comms booster module en route at mark 100. Hold at your target co-ordinates for further instructions."

"We've no indication of their military capability, of course, though that defence grid shows that they've at least got into space," Benson says when the Major gets back to him. He makes no comment about the Major's profligacy with the relay booster. "We're just stuck here playing the waiting game."

"The worst part." The Major watches the command console monitors for a moment or two, the ones showing the fighter/scout ships lined up ready in the launch tubes. An instant later and the first one rockets down its tube and is gone.

"Who've you sent out?" Benson's watching too. He folds his arms over his chest in a way I can't help feeling is apprehensive. Nervous. At least it means he keeps his hands to himself.

"Thom Aronsson's squad, Blue 3. Where's Blue2 now?" Harrington's still at the telemetry desk, staring at the screens.

"Sitting back by the sixth planet, trying to relay everything through to us," Benson starts, but he breaks off when the Comms officer leaps up.

"Got it, sir! Calvert's jury-rigged the relay. Coming through loud and clear!"

"On screen," Benson orders. "Someone tell the Commander we've got the link live. Record it in case we lose it." He glances at Harrington and grins. "She'll roast our nuts if she misses it."

We all stare at the big screens at the front of the bridge. This isn't the first time we've had contact with an alien race since we ran away from the Devourers, but it has to be three years since the last one. They'd been bombed back into the stone age centuries before we got there, so it hadn't exactly been an enlightening encounter.

All I can see of the alien is the upper torso, the exposed skin a gleaming copper. It's broadly humanoid in shape, at any rate, although the hairless head looks rather larger than we humans are used to, and when it raises a hand... well, I'll call it a hand, although there were far more fingers than I'm used to, they're too long and some of them writhe like snakes. There seems to be thin, semi-translucent webbing between some of those long fingers, too. The face, though, has the same sort or arrangement as ours, dominated by large eyes with vertical pupils, like a cat's. No nose, although two dark lines running down the centre of the face where a nose would be on a human, suggest nostril slits. High cheekbones and a well-shaped mouth.

I catch my breath and stare. I'm not the only one—the bridge is loud with gasps and mutters.

Because for all its strangeness, its eldritch eeriness, this alien is beautiful.

Very beautiful, in a terrible, terrifying way.

We're quiet for a long time, watching. The silence is broken only by the occasional report from one of the desks, or quiet status updates from Telemetry or Weapons.

"Some sort of public broadcasting?" I say, because it looks like a planetary vid system of some kind, the sort that we used to pick up from the Earth's colonies. God alone knows what the programmes might be about if my guess is right.

"Could be," Harrington says. "Looks boring enough for it."

My console pings at me. "The Commander's shuttle just landed."

The sound kicks in. The alien's mouth is moving, and a stream of incomprehensible liquid humming resonates in the speakers. It reminds me of birdsong.

We all turn to look at the Comms officer, who looks back at us, entranced, a small smile on her face as she listens to the alien. She makes a general announcement. "The computers are working on it. It's a complex language, and it's likely that the nuances are sub-vocal. That'll make it harder for us to interpret. It may be hours before we have a workable vocabulary, and even then, the finer grammatical rules may be beyond us."

She sounds delighted at the prospect.

"Thank you, Ensign," Benson says. He waits until she's turned back to the Comms desk before dabbing at the Major, who has evidently wandered in too close, saying, quietly, "Sub-vocal?"

"Body language?" Harrington suggests. "That's cultural, and the translation computers had a hard enough time coping with that within Earth and her colonies, much less a bunch of aliens."

"For all I know she could mean anything from semaphore to pheromones to ESP. I hate to ask. Let's hope they crack it before I send you down there, Major."

Now that makes me perk up, because if Major Harrington is going down there, that means I'll be going too.

"Why me?"

And that makes me perk up even more, because Harrington's tone isn't right. It isn't right at all. He doesn't sound like he's joking. He sounds tired. Tired and unenthusiastic. That isn't him.

Benson's fingers brush lightly over the insignia on Harrington's shoulder. "Remember when they gave you this, they promised you a life of glory and heroism and adventure?"

"Yeah."

"They were lying. Combat majors get all the

119

crap jobs."

"I'd noticed," is all the Major has time to say before Bekele sweeps out of the elevators, demanding updates. Everyone falls over themselves to respond, and maybe it's because I'm the only one who doesn't need to jump up and rattle out a status report (she's not that interested in shuttles even when we aren't on alert, and they slip down her priority list into invisibility when we are) that I have the attention to spare to see that Matt Harrington rubs a hand over his face to wipe away whatever he's worried is showing, before he salutes the Commander and gives his report.

"Full readiness, ma'am. Blue 2 made first contact and is relaying the transmission, and Blue 3 is on their way to get into the system from the other side. They'll be in position in"—Harrington glances at his watch—"three minutes. The rest of Blue squadron and Green are in the tubes on Alpha and Beta decks respectively. Red's on standby on Alpha, with their ships ready to swing into the tubes the minute Blue is clear. Yellow's on picket duty around our perimeter and reports that everything's quiet. Captain Merton has the infantry on Beta deck with the armoured shuttles ready to go. Gunners all report laser canon are charged and ready, our gun ports open."

Bekele has her gaze fixed on the screen. "Good." She gets into the command chair in the centre of the bridge by feel, she's so focused, reaching blindly behind her with one hand to guide herself in. "Good. Keep the status reports coming."

We all turn back to watching the screen. Talking heads stuff. I'm pretty sure now that it's some form of public broadcasting.

Bekele glances at the Comms desk. "What else are we monitoring?"

"The full frequency spectrum, ma'am. We can't work out which frequencies take their military traffic yet, not until the computers crack the language and give us a useable translator."

She nods, frowning.

I point to the screen. "I swear that's a weather report."

"Some things are truly universal." Benson is a sententious bastard. "Those symbols look ominous. If I was back home on Triton, I'd be hunting out the waterproofs."

"That's why they called it Triton." It's all I can do not to snort. "The place was bloody wet. I did a supply run there once and got mildew."

"But it was home," Benson says, and sighs.

I almost feel sorry for him. This is the only home we have now, and God alone knows if ever we'll find another. Not yet, anyway. Bekele's no fool and she wants more space between us and the Devourers before she'll allow landfall and colonisation. A lot more space. I can see us living this long exodus for years. His sigh brings me up short, too, reminding me of those nights I wake sweating from nightmares of the moment the Devourers reached my home planet and Mars was destroyed. I nod and make a noise that someone with a more generous heart than me would possibly define as sympathetic.

Benson straightens his shoulders. "Work first, Miss Li. Maudlin sentimentality on your own time."

See? He's a pompous bastard.

I turn back to the aliens and watch them for the next hour. They're more interesting than Benson and I am less tempted to space them. The transmission changes while I watch, and by the end of it there are more aliens on the screen: bi-pedal, two armed, all hairless and all of them a glowing coppery colour or bronze or gold. If more than one gender is represented on screen, they don't appear to dress in any sort of gendered way.

"Anything on the language yet?" Bekele sounds impatient. She runs a hand through her tight, greying curls and eases her shoulders. Maybe the tension's getting to her.

The Comms officer shakes her head. "We have some rudimentary vocabulary, ma'am. Maybe enough to pass the time of day."

"Keep working on it."

"Commander! Long range scanners indicate a multiple launch from the planet's surface. Six ships, ma'am."

"Warn Blue and Green leaders, please," Bekele

says without a hint of any emotion. "Prepare to launch."

She's the business, is Bekele. Nothing fazes her and her calm is monolithic. If you could distil it down, you'd be able to build bomb shelters out of it.

She glances at Harrington. "Launch all fighters."

"Launch Blue and Green," Harrington orders into his headset. There's barely a beat between her orders and his. "Red into the tubes and report when ready." A slight pause. "Blue's away, ma'am. And Green."

She nods. She's turned her eyes from the transmission to watch the screens above the telemetry desk, and that's her focus now.

"Patch me through to them." The Major's over by the navigation desk, and his order is for the Comms officer. "Blue and Green Squadrons, this is Harrington. Proceed to co-ordinates 34.66 by 465 by 82.3 alpha and await further orders. Captain Rosens, you have overall command until further notice." He waits for Rosens' acknowledgement. "Blue 3 leader, copy."

Thom Aronsson's tinny voice responds almost

immediately. "Here, sir."

"Move up to support Blue 2. Report when you're in position. Launch control, where's Red?"

"Going into the tubes now, Major."

"Good. Launch Red, and give them a rendezvous course to join the others at the holding point. Comms, patch me through to Captain Markham in Yellow."

"Commander! Unknowns will reach contact point with Blue2 in three minutes." The scanner officer's voice is thin. Strained.

Bekele is still calm and quiet. "I see. Go to red alert. Communications, warn the ships that we're about to make a first contact."

The bridge lights flash red, and klaxons sound again, high pitched enough to bore holes in your eardrums.

"Markham, we're on red. Keep the ships from scattering. Patch into channel fifty-six and you'll be able to monitor what's going down. Harrington out." The Major's watching the Telemetry screens and the tiny transponder dots that show his fighters are heading out to support Kit Calvert. "Liang, tell the ground crews to get my fighter ready."

"Already done, Major. Your ship's ready to go." Did he really think I wouldn't have that under control?

He gives me a quick, tight grin.

Kit Calvert's voice on the Comms system is surprisingly calm. "Can you see them, *Alexander*?"

We've got his transmission on line. The alien ships are bigger than our fighters, coming up fast, sleek and silvery where they catch the light of the system's sun.

"Defensive posture only, Blue2." Harrington's going for imitating Bekele's calm, speaking quietly over the link. "Defend yourselves if necessary."

"Don't worry. We will!"

"They're transmitting!" the Comms officer shouts, excitement making her voice crack.

"They've taken up a holding pattern ten kilometres away," Kit Calvert reports, the first note of tension in his voice. "Scanners read them as armed, but I think their gun ports are closed."

"Comms!" Bekele turns her head briefly to look at the Comms desk.

"Repeated transmission. No threatening cadences. Could be a standard greeting, ma'am."

How the hell can the Comms officer know that?

"Translation?"

The Comms officer shakes her head. "Sorry, Commander. We still don't have it."

"Blue, Green and Red squadrons at the holding point, ma'am," Harrington tells the Commander.

She just nods.

It's Benson who betrays his stress. "Where's that bloody translation?"

"I can't get— Wait! I've got something coming through now. But it's not ours! Commander, it's not ours. It's coming from them. They're transmitting in standard English. Here we go." The Comms officer hits a button on the console and puts it on audio.

"…in peace. We greet you. We welcome all those who come to us in peace. We greet you. We welcome all those who come to us in peace. We greet you…."

I only realise I'm sagging in my seat when my spine comes up against the back of my chair. They sound friendly, and oh! that's good. That's really good.

"Can we respond?" Bekele asks.

The Comms officer nods. "Their translations systems are powerful, ma'am. Standard good wishes response?"

"Yes." Bekele looks at Benson and her smile is controlled. Tight. "Yes. Tell them that we do indeed come in peace and we're looking forward to talking with them more fully."

"Done, ma'am."

A moment's wait, and the incoming message changes. There is a studiously ceremonial politeness about the voice that comes through the speakers, as their good wishes are reciprocated. The sort of ceremonial politeness that is so necessary to avoid misunderstandings.

"Major."

"Ma'am?"

"Join Blue2, please. Time to open negotiations."

Poor Matt Harrington. He always has to be first in, to take the risks for the people sitting fearfully in their metal ships. The ones who depend on him.

"I'm on my way."

"Don't worry, Major," Benson says. "We'll have worked out the sub-vocals by the time you get there."

"If you haven't, sir, I'll just have to fall back on semaphore."

Belling snorts. "You'd be better off spacing Calvert and waving him around a bit."

"Sir?"

"Pheromones, Major. They work every time."

It's just at that point that I turn to wish him luck, and I see the Major's face. I haven't seen anyone look like that for a long time. Hurt, loss and pain all have their teeth in him, worrying him. Someone has really kicked Matt Harrington's puppy.

My breath catches in my throat. Oh no.

Matt Harrington manages a very wry grin. "Yeah. So I hear."

Shit.

"P'NAT'R? WITH APOSTROPHES? Seriously?" I roll my eyes.

Major Harrington's briefing us on this job. We're all sitting in the bridge conference room and by 'we' I mean the diplomatic team who'll be negotiating with these apostrophised people. And by 'diplomatic', I mean Benson, Harrington, Kit Calvert and Thom Aronsson, plus a couple of military units for escort, all of them under orders not to insert their combat boots into bodily orifices, and instead to speak sweetly to the nice aliens and see if they have anything we want that we can trade for.

Oh. And my co-pilot and me. At least I get to hold Alice's hand under the table as we listen to this stuff.

Apostrophes. Good grief.

"That's what the translator units say. Who am I to argue with the linguists?" Harrington tries to smile back, but it isn't sincere.

Well someone ought to argue. And check the linguists' reading matter. They have far too many space opera comics, obviously.

"The apostrophes represent something only linguists care about." And by now Harrington just sounds tired. "A glottal stop or voiceless phonation or something like that."

Well, that was me told. I wish I hadn't asked. I give it up at that point and focus on the rest of the briefing. Diplomacy. Trade negotiations. What we need in food stores and technology to eke out the half-lives of the refugees. Don't allow them to steal the *Alexander* from under us. Got it.

Two hours later I bring the shuttle in over the equator, skimming through the upper atmosphere, and into the northern hemisphere, up into the temperate zones. We do a lot of scanning on the way, plotting out their major cities and population centres, and trying to gather information about things like industrialisation, power generation, energy sources. All these things are grist to our diplomatic mill. Thom Aronsson's good at analysing that sort of thing. He's another of Harrington's captains. Another one chosen for his skills.

"It'll help us work out where we're ahead of them on the technological front and where we're behind, and what the P'Nat'r might want from us or what they have to offer," Thom says, as he charts an interesting-looking power grid radiating out from a large structure over to port.

You don't say.

But Thom's a good guy, and I don't say it aloud. He knows anyway, if the grin he sends my way is any indication.

A flight of six P'Nat'r ships take over escort duty from a Red squadron patrol, just beyond the planet's atmosphere. We sit through a few minutes of elaborate courtesies on the communications channel.

"They're a ceremonial people, Li Liang." Kit Calvert leans over the arm of my chair, listening to Harrington's civil nothings as he speaks to the P'Nat'r. "Try and be polite."

Obviously, he's never come across the concept of 'face', *mianzi*, 面子. It won't allow me to be anything else. I can't risk the safety and wellbeing of my team, to shirk my duty to them, and maintain face. I can, however, elbow him hard in the ribs to get him out of my personal space.

The breath whooshes out him in a very satisfactory way. I have sharp elbows.

When the shuttle has been handed over formally to the P'Nat'r escort, Major Harrington dismisses the Vipers. I watch them go, half apprehension and half excitement. Not too worried though. Sure, we're putting our trust in the notion that the P'Nat'r won't attack us. But, as Benson says, we'll need to show trust if we're to gain it.

Besides, none of the *Alexander*'s shuttles are unarmed, although with our gun ports closed the P'Nat'r won't—I hope— be able to gauge our military capability. We aren't toothless and I can have those ports open in less than a heartbeat.

"Fly carefully, Liang," Kit says, giving the P'Nat'r ships a long, careful look.

I give Kit a long, disdainful one, and bring the shuttle down at a spaceport outside what appears to be the P'Nat'r main city.

"Atmosphere checks out at almost Earth norm," Thom says. "About 20% oxygen. We might find some other gases a touch high. It'll smell different, that's for sure."

Which we'll notice, because we won't be wearing encounter suits. Apparently hiding our faces inside masks isn't diplomatic enough. When we get back, we'll be spending three weeks in quarantine as a result.

Hang diplomacy, I say. Quarantine is going to be hell.

The Major snorts. "The *Alexander* isn't all that fragrant."

Kit breaks in with a "Yeah, but that's just human bodies. What do we have here, Thomas, my son?" His tone is determinedly light. Insouciant.

Harrington half turns away from him. "Thom?"

"There's more sulphur in the air here, Major. It'll smell like fireworks."

Alice glances from Kit to the Major and makes a little grimace at me. Smells like fireworks in here, too.

Kit and Matt Harrington have seemed a bit stiff and unnatural with each other recently. Not quite a coolness. Just not as warm as usual. You have to look closely to see it, because Matt's always been a very private, discreet man.

Now he's discreet and cold with it.

A burned out firework, maybe. All char and ash.

MAYBE THE P'NAT'R ARE MADE out of some sort of metal. They're all golden or bronze or copper, and they almost shine. It's as if... Well, it's as if they don't just get up in the morning and shower, they get up in the morning and get themselves *polished*.

They sort of glow.

You can tell, straight off, that the P'Nat'r aren't human. They glow and they're tall and glittering and every damn one of them is beautiful. Even to human eyes, they're beautiful. There's no one who's short or plain—no buck teeth, spots or frizzy hair for the P'Nat'r, no sir. No one who can't see or hear or walk. Nothing but perfect, beautiful almost-human-looking people.

It makes my teeth ache, all that perfection. Matt Harrington says they're enough to give humanity a permanent inferiority complex.

"Well, they're sure as Hades giving me some sort of complex," Thom mutters. "You know, I'll put up with a lot for the refugee ships. I'll put up with a lot because it's my duty as a soldier. I'll put up with a lot because I know that they have stuff we could use and a trade deal can only help everyone up there. But the next P'Nat'r who runs over to me to pinch me, stroke me or touch my hair, and I swear I'll will bite him. Or her."

I grimace with him. We've been here five days now, and I get how frustrated he is. Kit, though, just laughs. He has a habit of not letting things get him down. Especially other people's things.

The Major doesn't laugh. "They're not what I'd describe as diverse."

Because along with not having anyone who doesn't reach some humanly-unreachable standard of perfection, they don't appear to have more than one ethnicity. Now that's their fatal flaw, in my view, but there's no knowing what they think about it.

"Unless," the Major says, "the racial differences are between gold, bronze and copper."

"That's a thought." But Thom remains glum.

It's possible that the Major is right. The golden ones have golden glowing skin and toning gold hair and eyes a tawny yellow; the bronze and coppery ones have the same sort of all-over colouration, just different shades. That might mean they're three different ethnic groupings, but the differences between them aren't marked. The thing for sure is that they don't have anyone like Thom or me, and much as they're interested in humans generally, they've been fascinated by that difference. Particularly with Thom.

Thom really, really doesn't like it, I know. He's been stared at, openly. I've seen them talk to each other, huddled in whispers, pointing at him. He's even had P'Nat'r run up to him and rub his hand or arm with their long thin fingers, as if they think he's tarnished and the colour will come off if they rub hard enough. Okay, only kids did that and their parents pulled them away really quickly, but still. Thom has a right to complain. Seriously, though, it's just as well Bekele isn't down here as well, because she would not tolerate being patted and prodded. She'll come down when we have something to sign, some positive outcome of the mission, and we're all praying the P'Nat'r will have got over themselves before she arrives.

"I feel like something in a zoo," Thom says. So far, though, he's just grinned and borne it.

"Bite," I remind him.

Harrington stops and turns. He looks serious. "Are you getting too uncomfortable with it?"

"I wouldn't mind if we all got the same level of attention. They got over you and the others pretty fast and Kit...well, if it wasn't for his blue eyes, the bastard would fit right in with them."

Which is true. Thom Aronsson may have the Scandinavian name, but Kit Calvert has the typical golden colouring. The P'Nat'r have loved that.

"Yes," the Major says, and his mouth twists a little. It's only for the most fleeting second, but it's there.

"I don't like being treated like some sort of exotic animal, Major. It's demeaning."

He nods. "I know. I feel bad about it."

"Just so long as you do."

Major Harrington gives Thom a small grin, but it's sympathetic. "And I know that even with what the anthropologists say about it being the natural curiosity of a truly homogenous race, it has to feel intrusive."

"Yeah." Thom waves his free hand around, continuing the conversation. "And those pontificating anthropologists are where, exactly?"

The Major chuckles. "Never where you want them."

"Never down here to deal with any of that natural curiosity first hand. Bastards."

"All scientists are bastards," I say, and Thom turns to glower at me and accuse me of sounding far too cheerful about it.

Harrington tugs him onward. "We're off to a festival, people, so let's all just relax and forget about all the shit we have to deal with. I've left 'the Major' back in our quarters. The name's Matt tonight, remember? We're off duty."

As if he'd ever be off duty. Not really.

It's been a long day of periods of intense negotiation interspersed with cultural stuff: visits to art galleries and so on. The P'Nat'r are intent on displaying their culture to us, and already we'd seen a lot of their visual art, architecture. Even performing arts. The previous evening we'd been taken to, well, I can only call it opera. The timbre and pitch of the singing were not geared to the human ear and although the sound was eerily beautiful, paradoxically it was not attractive.

Tonight it's a festival of some sort.

We're walking slowly through a great open park beside a river. It's twilight and the light is an odd greeny-mauve and where the shadows are gathering under the tall vegetation that isn't quite trees, the mauve deepens to a dark purple. We've got used to the normal smell of the air, and here there's something more, something stronger. A more pleasant, sweeter smell. Here and there white flowers gleam in the dusk.

Under its biodomes, Mars was once scented twilight, just like this and flowers grew in the hydroponics gardens. Maybe not quite just like this, but close.

Now Mars is dust and ashes.

There's no point thinking about that. Think about tonight instead. Put one foot in front of the other, just as the Skipper said back when it happened, and keep plodding on. It's a long walk to the middle of the park to reach the riverside and the place where the P'Nat'r hold this festival we're being taken to. The park is vast, despite being in the centre of the city. We've been walking for nearly half-an-hour and I still can't see the river.

One foot in front of the other, Li Liang. One step at a time.

There are hundreds of P'Nat'r walking near us, strolling along pathways edged with tiny white lights. Not with us, just near us. Our guide is just ahead with Kit and Benson, but there's a bit of space between the human group and the P'Nat'r around us.

Not that it stops them staring, of course.

I hold Alice's hand tighter as the stares rake over us.

Jilmara, our guide today, has realised we've dropped behind and is jogging back towards us. Matt tucks his arm through Thom's and starts us all off again, smiling reassurances to Jilmara. Alice and I switch up a gear to keep up. Thom notices, and holds Matt back until Alice and I catch them up.

I'm not sure why Matt's hanging back from the main group, but he's not in any hurry to catch up. Except... yes, Kit. That would do it. Kit's in the group ahead of us, and Matt doesn't want to be. Once or twice Kit looks back at us and grins, but he's brown-nosing Benson for some reason and doesn't have time for the rest of us tonight. It's quite something watching him turn on the charm like that and watching Benson, the poor sap, respond to it, turning to him to bask in his attention.

Alice's hold on my hand tightens. "What's up with them?" she asks, very quietly. We've known about Matt and Kit for years. Only now it doesn't look like there is a Matt and Kit.

I shrug. I haven't heard any gossip. Which in itself is probably significant.

Benson turns just then and calls Matt forward. Matt's grimace is probably not visible to Benson, but none of us miss it. Major Harrington jogs forward to catch up our revered Exec Officer, not Matt. Matt's retreated again, hiding behind his rank.

Thom swears, softly, half under his breath. Alice and I exchange looks and move one each side Thom, linking arms with him. He needs comfort, does Thom. He's carried that particular torch for a long time.

Out of nowhere, Thom says, "Kit and Matt split up last month. Finally, I mean. They've always had a funny sort of thing going and I never really could understand it. I think the split's been coming for a long time. Kit's been playing the field, and Matt won't put up with that crap. Kit says he's thinking about moving in with Helen Spears. Know her?"

"She's in Engineering," Alice says at once. "Aerospace propulsions system specialist."

"That's the one." Thom's tone is flat, which tells me what he thinks about it. "Kit told me earlier today he was getting serious with her."

Kit looks back at us again and grins. He knows we're talking about him, because it's like all rivers running to the sea: all conversations in Kit's world are about him. Sadly, in this case he's right.

"Matt?"

"Hasn't said anything much. He doesn't show much, either."

I nod, because that's true. If Kit Calvert's all about what's sparkling on the surface, Matt Harrington is deep, quiet places. "What did you say to Kit?"

Thom shrugs. "Not a lot. Only asked him if it's really what he wants, and it is, apparently."

"Me, I'd have asked him if he's blind or stupid—but he is, apparently." Although to be honest, if it wasn't for Alice, I'd have quite liked Helen Spears myself. And if it wasn't for the fact Helen's straight.

Thom lets out a snort. "Sometimes, I think Kit's actually pretty damn stupid."

"I thought you liked him?" Alice sounds surprised. "You've been friends for ever."

"I do. It's just—" Thom shrugs again. "Not always, no. I don't always like him. He's a selfish bastard some days. Matt didn't deserve what Kit dished out there. Kit gets away with too much shit."

I know what he means. Kit has a cheeky nonchalance, an insouciance, a sort of emotional independence that can bite like acid. And yet he's always smiling and charming, everyone's best buddy.

He has people acting like… what had my mother called them?

"Girasoles, that's it." I say.

Thom and Alice both stare at me, but only Thom speaks. "What?"

Alice only smiles, and because she knows me better than I do myself, she just waits.

"Girasoles. Sunflowers. My mother told me about those big yellow flowers that grew on Earth, the ones that turned their faces to the sun and followed it across the sky. Doesn't it piss you off when everyone treats Kit as their sun?"

Thom looks startled, eyes a little wide, but he laughs. A short laugh with not much joy in it. "Oh, yes. I know what you mean. That's another reason not to like Kit today."

Alice's smile widens. "But to be honest, mostly we love him."

"Yeah, the self-centred bastard," Thom says, and shakes his head, smiling. "Mostly we do."

I lean back to glance at Alice behind his back. She nods and snuggles in to Thom's side, and I do the same. The chill of the evening air is warded off by the warmth of Thom between us.

THE FESTIVAL OF Winterlight, Jilmara tells us, is about preparing for the coming of winter and the renewal of life and faith to face the darkening days.

I stop and stare.

We're standing at one end of a long low table holding hundreds of little lanterns made of something that looks like thin tissue paper stretched on a sturdy wire frame. Some are plain bright colours, others painted with designs and the flowing P'Nat'r script. There's a little tin dish in the centre of each lantern's base and piles of small round waxy cakes set along the table's length. There are dozens of tables scattered around the river bank, and hundreds and hundreds of lanterns. More hang on the branches of the not-quite-trees.

No.

No, it's not possible.

"Liang? What is it?" Alice tugs at my arm. "Liang?"

元宵节

"Yuánxiāojié." Even to my own ears, my voice is a thread. I'm breathing too hard, pulling in the air with a low gasp on every quickening breath. "It's Yuánxiāojié. But it can't be! It can't be."

Matt looms up at my side, Thom beside him. I can only stare and breathe, and blink the hot stinging out of my eyes.

Beside each lantern is a square of red paper and a square of cream, and a long thin stick of something that might be, but probably isn't, charcoal. I touch one. It doesn't get all over my fingers. No, not charcoal. The Lords forbid that a P'Nat'r would get grubby. That'd seriously interfere with perfection.

Matt's arm is around my shoulders. "Take it easy, Liang. What's ywen-sshyaoww…" He pauses, and grimaces. At any other time I'd laugh at the way he's murdering Mandarin, but not tonight. I can't laugh at that tonight.

"You don't understand. This is Yuánxiāojié, the Lantern Festival. It's just the same." I clutch at the front of his jacket. "Matt, how can this be the same?"

Benson's there, at Matt's shoulder. "What the hell, Major?" His voice is low, hard. He glares at me. "You're embarrassing our hosts, Li."

Jilmara tilts her head towards me. It's odd to see her mouth move into shapes I can't recognise and emit sounds like birdsong, and yet to hear, an instant later, her fluting, musical English come from the translator we all wore on our wrists. "This is familiar to you, Li Liang?"

I work my mouth for a moment before I can speak, it's so dry. "Where I'm from, in my culture, we have the Lantern Festival. Not at the beginning of winter, but at the end of our New Year festival, to celebrate the coming spring…" I break off.

"Ah, so our festivals stand at each end of winter, enclosing it between them? Interesting. Tell me of yours, Li Liang."

So I ignore Benson's glowering presence and tell her of the days spent celebrating New Year, and how 元宵节, Yuánxiāojié, the Lantern Festival is the sending-off celebration for family members who travelled to the countryside to celebrate the new year and now must return to their lives in the cities. I tell her of the myriad lanterns of all shapes and sizes filling the streets and shops, many of them red for good luck; how we'd paste riddles onto them and give little prizes to anyone who guessed the answers; and how we'd celebrate with traditional dancing and food before lighting our lanterns and letting them float free to carry our love for our families and our wishes for a prosperous and happy New Year into the future.

"And much good that did us," I say at the end, but quietly. Perhaps only Matt and Alice hear me, because Matt pats my shoulder and Alice wraps me up in her arms to keep me safe. Thom stands stolid behind me and even Kit looks subdued.

"Here," Jilmara says, "we are preparing ourselves for the long darkness, purifying ourselves as our gods demand. First, we write all our fears and hates and doubts onto red paper. Then we write all our hopes and wishes onto cream paper and put that paper here, into this slit in a lantern. See?" She picks up a lantern and shows us. "And then we use the rolled-up red paper to light the fuel in the reservoirs here, and let the lanterns float up into the sky. We release them all at same time and fill the sky with hope, while we've burned away all the things holding us back. It lets us enter winter with courage, cleansed of doubts and fears."

There's a second or two before Benson rushes to fill the silence with lots of diplomatic nodding and smiles and several variations on *What a fascinating festival!* Jilmara nods, and with a graceful bow, walks off with Benson and Kit in close attendance. She stops to speak with another P'Nat'r, and they both turn to look at me.

"Confession was nowhere near as much fun as that," Thom says, very quietly.

"Maybe you can convert," I say.

Thom laughs. "I just stopped going to confession."

We all laugh at his wry tone. Kit, standing a few

feet away at Benson's right hand, turns and gives us a strange look. Probably doesn't like it when people enjoy themselves without his sparkling personality there to help. Maybe he'd rather be with his friends than sucking up to the great and the good, but he's chosen his bed. Let him lie in it. Matt deserves better.

I catch myself up there because, seriously, what's the point of being mad with Kit because he's Kit? That's like being mad with rain because it's wet. Kit's all right, really. Just too charming for his own good. I grin at him, until I get a smile back.

Thom gives my shoulders a little shake. "All right, now?"

"Yes." And I am, smiling into the dimming evening at the people who, I realise, I have come to love as my family. I'm going to pretend this is Yuánxiāojié and I'm spending it as tradition asks of me, sharing with those I love. "It was just the shock."

Jilmara returns then and bows to me again. "I have spoken to one in authority, Li Liang. She has given me permission to amend our ceremony tonight and combine it with yours as far as I can. Since red is the colour of good luck for your people, write your fears and hates onto the cream paper, and your hopes onto the red. That way, we can celebrate together."

She doesn't let me speak when I try to get my voice out past the lump that's solid in my throat, but she touches my lips with one many-fingered hand while the other coils the more tentacle-y fingers around mine. Her hands are soft, and warm, and the shock of feeling too many fingers entwined with mine is overcome by her generosity.

"Come," she says, and leads us to the nearest table. "Write."

Though I take my place at the table, it's a few minutes before my eyes clear enough for me to write anything at all.

I write using the ancient pictograms of my ancestors. This is not my people's festival, not entirely, but it's the closest I will ever come to it. Never again will I see the red lanterns of Yuánxiāojié. Never again. I am the last to celebrate it, and so every step, every moment, should be filled with the significance of who and what I am. I embody the old ways tonight, brought to life for the very last time.

I tighten my grip on the writing stick and take a deep breath. My fingertips hold the cream paper square in place.

Fears and hates and doubts. I can do that.

I write that Alice is beside me, her side pressed up against mine and that when she turns her head, her hair brushes against my cheek. It smells of herbs. I write that I'm too afraid to guess what her fears are, and far too afraid to guess at her hopes because they might, just might, not match mine and I'd rather not know. I write that I'm afraid, that I'm almost ten years older than she is, and that one day she'll grow older, wiser, restless. That the best I can do is hold on to her for as long as she's willing to be held, and store up enough grace to let her go when the times comes. I can write that, because I fear it above everything.

I could write that I'm afraid we'll never find a haven, and that I'll die rootless and wandering. But truth be told, as long as I'm with the friends who are all the family I have now, perhaps that doesn't matter so much. We all die. Where we do it, isn't so big a deal. But it gives me something to write, so that goes onto the paper.

I could write that I hate the Devourers for everything they've done, but no putting little spills of paper to the flame will purge me of that. Every one of us will be writing that tonight, and none of us will be rid of it. That's one to burn in the nights when I can't sleep and Earth's dust and ashes threaten to choke me. Still, it might lift a little of the guilt of not having died with everyone else, and that will be worth it. So, I write that, too, slashing the pictograms onto the paper in hard, black strokes.

Beside me Thom is writing. I wonder what he's thinking? That sometimes he doubts he'll ever be visible, when Kit's around, because Kit is the one who makes Matt smile? That he hates it when Matt is as helpless in Kit's thrall as the rest of us? That Kit really is stupid to throw Matt away for someone else?

"Do I need to get a psych report done on you, Thom?" asks Matt, who's on Thom's other side. "You're writing an awful lot there."

"Sunflowers." Thom says aloud, and underlines the word. He glances up and looks first at me. We nod at each other, and then he turns to Matt and smiles.

Matt blinks. "Sunflowers. Are they a fear, a hate or a doubt?"

Thom folds his cream paper, running his thumbnail down the creases. "All three."

I've known for a long time, years, that Thom doesn't just want what Kit is too careless to keep, although he does. He really wants Matt to look at him, the way that Matt looks at Kit. He wants to be visible.

I know this because I'm nosy and I see things, and I love Thom like a brother. I see what he writes when, finally, he picks up his square of red paper.

He writes only two letters on the red square before folding it and slipping it into his lantern.

MY FINGERS ARE white on the writing stick, clenched so hard they ache as painfully as hope aches in my heart.

心爱 and 安全 and 找到家

Xīn'ài. Ānquán. Zhaodao jia.

Beloved. Safety. Find home.

The red paper is thick, hard to fold. But it slips into my lantern all the same. embracing hope, holding the future within it though written in the picture-letters of the past.

THE P'NAT'R ARE IN a happy mood, relaxed and carefree. Children are forming rings, holding hands and dancing, laughing and sweet and dizzy with excitement. That's something they have in common with humans, then. It's reassuring.

They bring us food and drink in abundance, and all along the river bank, great torches are burning in metal baskets, like little bonfires in the sky. The big clearing is lit up by them and even though it's fully dark now, I can see the reddish-green of foliage against the sky. Odd how on every planet, some things are not quite the same, but recognisable. Similar. Here the clearing is ringed with not-quite trees covered in not-quite leaves. I don't know what else to call them. They're pretty, anyway.

"The children will come and light your lanterns," Jilmara says. "Because they are our greatest hope."

I put a little waxy cake of fuel into the tin reservoir at the bottom of my lantern, roll my cream parchment into a tight cylinder of compressed hate and fear, and wait. It's getting chilly. That's why I'm shivering.

A bronze child appears before me, popping up out of the deepening darkness, Jilmara beside him. The young one has a taper in his hand, glowing at the end, and with Jilmara's encouragement, reaches up to touch it to the end of the rolled cream parchment. When that catches, the little one shows me how to light the cake of fuel in my lantern, his flawless face creased with concentration as he performs this ceremonial duty for a guest from another world.

"Wait on the signal," Jilmara says, when we're all ready, holding her own lantern in front of her.

There's nothing to do but push the remains of my fears and hates and doubts into the little cake of wax. The fuel is burning brightly, flames licking upwards. It's astonishing that the whole lantern doesn't go up. But none of them do. They never did back home, either, when my whole community came together for this. My hands warm and I shift my grip on the lantern, keeping it gentle so as not to bend the wire frame.

The crowd's quiet now, waiting.

"Any moment now," Jilmara murmurs, and laughs when, an instant later, a firework streaks across the sky to burst over the river in a shower of silver and scarlet and green. "Now!"

I let my hands part when she speaks. The lantern stutters for a second, wavering from side to side, then the hot air from the wax tablet does its work and the lantern rises, ever more steadily, with dozens and dozens of other lanterns beside it. My lantern bumps gently into

Alice's and lifts up.

The sky is filled with lanterns, nudging into each other like too many boats in a harbour bobbing on the incoming tide. There's a moment of deep silence, and I let it sink in.

"Yuánxiāojié kuàilè!" I say, and kiss Alice. "Happy Lantern Festival."

"I think that's the most beautiful thing I've seen," Matt says.

I turn to him. Matt's looking up at the sky, his profile etched against the flaring light of the torches and a sky filled with hope.

Thom looks at me, and smiles, before turning back to study Matt. Thom isn't looking up at the sky at all.

"Yes," he says. "I've always thought so."

KIT BOUNCES UP TO US, of course, when the silence is broken with cheers and lots of voices raised in laughter and singing. The children start up again, running and dancing.

"So," he says, "What did you all wish for?"

"You mustn't tell," Jilmara says, before any of us could speak. "You must never tell, or it won't happen."

I wouldn't have told, anyway. Somehow that isn't what Kit is for, to tell your hopes and wishes to. Not everything should be used for jokes and laughter. Kit has the disappointed look of a kid who's had his candy twitched out of his grasp.

"What about if you know what someone else has wished for, anyway?" I ask. "Know just by chance, I mean. Will it happen then?"

"Then it is your duty to try and make the wish and hope come true, Li Liang. More than a duty—a pleasure. It is a good thing to do. It is an honour to know such a secret; a greater honour to help bring it to fruition."

I nod. "Yes. It would be pleasing. And it's something that's just... right. Right for everyone."

The festival imbues everything tonight, colours my every thought. I will do what I can for Matt and Thom. For my family.

"You lot are boring," Kit says, laughing. He bounces away again, pulling Jilmara along with him. "Come on, there's food and singing and dancing. I want to dance."

Benson turns to follow him, scrambling after him, not wanting to be left behind. He looks the least fussy and the most relaxed I've ever seen him. I wonder what his hopes and fears were.

We watch as Kit leads Jilmara into a ring of children and is shown how to do the dance. The P'Nat'r become little sunflowers too. At least they're the right colours for it; gold and bronze and copper, all following that Kit-ian sun's progress. Their parents stand around laughing and clapping, eyes all fixed on Kit.

Matt's laugh is fond. Amused. "How does he do that, do you think? Makes himself the centre of everything that goes on, I mean."

"Girasoles," Thom says.

And I nod. Because they're all stupid, stupid, stupid. They can't see they're being dazzled.

"Ah, your sunflowers." Matt's smiling now. "Why sunflowers?"

"With Kit as the sun."

Matt tilts his head. His eyes widen a fraction, and he nods. "Yeah, I guess that sort of works. He does like to be the centre of everyone's attention."

Alice grips my hand, hard. When I look at her, she gives Thom and Matt a nod, arching her eyebrows at me. I grin, and she rolls her eyes.

"I don't know how to stop revolving around him," Thom says. "It's like moths to a candle flame."

"Does it bother you that much?"

"Hell, yes. It's being shown the wires and the illusions, and still falling for the magician's trick, every time. It's stupid, seeing yourself being dazzled and letting it happen anyway."

I tug on Alice's hand and put a little space

between us, and Matt and Thom. Giving them space.

"It used to bother me, too," Matt says. "A lot when... before, I mean."

"Are you saying it doesn't bother you now?"

"Less, I think. I've found some anchors. It twists you less, if you're anchored down." Matt gestures at the night with one hand. "What we do to keep the refugee ships going, to keep our people alive. That anchors me. Hope, I guess, that we'll get through and find somewhere to start again."

"Anchors," Thom says. "Yes. Anchors and hope."

They're both quiet now. I look up into a dark sky, and beside me Alice sighs and leans her head against mine. The lanterns are little more than pricks of light now and many of them have gone out. Maybe the dark lanterns are drifting back to the ground, their little lights blown out. What happens to the hopes and wishes then? Are they blown out, too?

There's a little warmth behind my ribs. I don't think they're blown out. I think everything I want is floating up there, and one day I'll get it all. One day.

"I didn't write anything on my red paper," Alice says, soft in my ear. "I've got everything I need." Her hand squeezes mine.

It's hard to breathe. "Really?"

She points up with her free hand. "My Winterlight isn't up there, Liang. It's down here."

And now it's hard to speak. I can only nod, and wish we were alone so I could show her how much light she spills on me, that she's my sun and for her, I'm happy to be a sunflower.

"What did Thom write on his paper?" Alice's voice is a ghost in my ear. Her breath tickles.

"Someone's initials." I nod at Matt, but I doubt I really need to. Alice isn't stupid.

Her mouth is on my cheek, and I feel it curve upwards. "Good. Do you think Matt knows?"

We turn to look at them. Matt's standing close to Thom, their shoulders pressed together, and he's linked their arms. He says nothing, and he's still staring up into the sky at the fading lights. Thom's looking at him, a faint smile lifting the corners of his mouth. It makes my breath catch, the hopeful look on Thom's face.

Oh, I think Matt knows. Maybe Thom's more visible than he thinks.

I smile at Alice, and I watch her for a long time, taking my first few breaths in a new life of hope and promise, and letting her light anchor me.

心爱

Beloved.

ABOUT THE AUTHOR

You can contact me through my website - www.annabutlerfiction.com, where you'll find links to my facebook and Twitter pages - or at annabutlerfiction@gmail.com

I love space opera, with spaceships and laser pistols and humanity fighting for its survival against unknowable, unfathomable aliens and, at the same time, against itself and humans' own worst traits. Yes, I'm hopelessly old fashioned!

I am currently working on two, quite different, series of books:

- The *Taking Shield* series is classic science fiction with LGBT protagonists, set at a time when Earth went dark thousands of years before, and her last descendants don't even know where she is. They have problems of their own. Albion, Earth's last colony, has been at war with the Maess for three generations; a war the humans are coming to realize they can't win. This series of LGBT mainstream novels charts the life and loves of Shield Captain Bennet as he struggles to help ensure his people's survival.

Passing Strangers is a prequel to this series, telling of the destruction of Earth.

- The *Lancaster's Luck* series is a classic m/m romance, but with the added twist of a steampunk world where aeroships fill the skies of Victorian London and our hero uses pistols powered by luminferous aether and phlogiston.

To keep in touch with publication of new books in each series, you can follow my blog and sign up for my quarterly newsletter – both at
www.annabutlerfiction.com

Made in the USA
Charleston, SC
15 January 2017